THE ANTARCTICA OF LOVE

The
ANTARCTICA
of LOVE

SARA
STRIDSBERG

TRANSLATED FROM THE SWEDISH BY
DEBORAH BRAGAN-TURNER

FARRAR, STRAUS AND GIROUX   NEW YORK

Farrar, Straus and Giroux
120 Broadway, New York 10271

Printed in the United States of America
Originally published in Swedish in 2018 by Albert Bonniers Förlag, Sweden,
as *Kärlekens Antarktis*
English translation originally published in 2021 by MacLehose Press,
Great Britain
English translation published in the United States by Farrar, Straus and Giroux
First American edition, 2022

Library of Congress Cataloging-in-Publication Data
Names: Stridsberg, Sara, 1972– author. | Bragan-Turner, Deborah, translator.
Title: The Antarctica of love / Sara Stridsberg ; translated from the Swedish
by Deborah Bragan-Turner.
Other titles: Kärlekens Antarktis. English
Description: First American edition. | New York : Farrar, Straus and
Giroux, 2022. | "Originally published in Swedish in 2018 by Albert
Bonniers Förlag, Sweden, as Kärlekens Antarktis"
Identifiers: LCCN 2021019888 | ISBN 9780374272692 (hardcover)
Classification: LCC PT9877.29.T75 K3713 2021 | DDC 839.73/8—dc23
LC record available at https://lccn.loc.gov/2021019888

Our books may be purchased in bulk for promotional, educational, or
business use. Please contact your local bookseller or the Macmillan Corporate
and Premium Sales Department at 1-800-221-7945, extension 5442,
or by email at MacmillanSpecialMarkets@macmillan.com.

www.fsgbooks.com
www.twitter.com/fsgbooks • www.facebook.com/fsgbooks

1   3   5   7   9   10   8   6   4   2

The Antarctica of Love is a literary fantasy and all the characters in the novel are
fictional. Any resemblance to actual people or events is coincidental and derives
only from the reality of violence.

SWEDISH
ARTSCOUNCIL

The cost of this translation was defrayed by a subsidy from the Swedish Arts
Council, gratefully acknowledged.

CREATION

We were in the forest at this point. In a kind of twilight, but with no sun, a brownish rainy gloom settling over the scene. Could I have rung someone? No, I couldn't, because even if there had been someone to ring, time would have run out. Now there was just the fading, submerged light and the huge trees and giant raindrops falling from the branches like the tears of grotesquely large beings and the two of us, he and I, and the feeling so intense of being the only ones left in the world, a feeling no reality could have changed, no cars we encountered on the roads, no lit-up telephone boxes we drove past, no voice on the radio gently purring, preaching, intoning like a devotional chant. The sound brought little scrapbook pictures to my mind. Of the Virgin Mary with the great menacing angel. Of Mary with the chubby little baby that was wheeling around at her breast in every painting, without wings but still beyond gravity's pull. And finally of Mary alone, without her child, when he was gone from the earth.

I lay on the forest floor looking at the dark tree roots steadily pushing down into the lake water. Everything was so still even the most gradual of movements showed, the treetops swaying in slow motion high above, the insects crawling on the underside of every flower and the drops of water falling from the branches and breaking in a slowed-down splash against the earth, miniature pearls of reflection travelling through the air in an infinitely slow-moving arc. And now it was cold, and urine and blood and faeces ran down my legs. I was thinking that the trees must be suspended between man and God, stretching their crowns up to the heavens, their roots like dragons' talons clawing into the earth where the dead reside and where soon I would be.

It was too late to ask for help now, too late for praying, time was irretrievably up. He said: "Get on your knees." And I knelt in the black grass. He said: "I'm going to blindfold you now. It'll be easier that way," he said. "That's good," I said, wondering which of us it would be easier for. "Now I'm going to strangle you and you won't be able to say anything else."

"Do it," I said. "I have nothing to say in any case."

And now he cuts what is left of my body into seven pieces and stuffs the rest into two white suitcases. He throws my head into a slurry pit that has a surface the same pink colour as vomit. It is not very far from the lake, down a little path through the wood; he has worked everything out on an old orienteering map. He stands for a while staring out over the thick bubbling mass before he drops it carefully into the sludge. Green and black flies and shimmering dragonflies zigzag across the surface as my head sinks slowly to the bottom, not very deep, just a few metres. My dark hair spreads out like a black parachute above me until my head comes to rest where no-one will ever find it, for it will soon be eaten away by chemicals. That picture keeps coming back to me, my hair in the water, reaching upwards as my head strikes the bottom, before settling.

*

And then? He walks back along the path. The sun is on its way down on the far side of the lake. A gentle rain falls on the forest. I have always loved rain. Always – how brief that was. How brief life was.

I mean to let your world be, but suddenly I find myself looking in again. It has such beauty from a distance, the fragile, iridescent blue of the atmosphere surrounding your planet, slightly impaired but still there. Beneath it there are clouds drifting slowly over the sky that is yours and bare autumn trees reaching out for sunlight, and further down still the black water streaming into Stockholm from the sea, glistening dark and oily between the islands, just the odd fallen leaf dotted on the surface. A world as motionless as an old oil painting at the National Museum. Only when you come close do you see there is movement down there, the aeroplanes and birds in their sky, human beings on their earth, worms crawling through the flowers and the eyes of the dead.

I try to concentrate on things that don't hurt. A child walking down the street, holding on to a balloon, unable to stop looking up all the time at its wondrousness. I watch rabbits playing in the grass at night outside the major hospitals. I often watch the light, at it constantly changing like refractions in a kaleidoscope. It affords me a kind of solace. Sometimes I watch two people making love; it is bad manners, there is no doubt, but nobody notices I am there and I think there is something beautiful in the way they cling to one another. I often look into hospital wards when a child comes flying in from eternity and alights at her mother's breast. I always love that moment when everything is still perfectly intact between a mother and her child. The other day, at first light, I saw a youth stop to help an old woman who had collapsed in a drunken stupor in the park at Björn's garden. When he lifted her up from the ground, she draped her arms around his neck like a child who had fallen asleep. Before he left her, they shared a cigarette and laughed about something I couldn't hear. But I saw the fear in her lacklustre blue eyes gradually give way to a faint glow; I saw her worn-out old soul light up in the first rays of sun. I avoid looking at evil wherever possible. I have already seen evil.

Someday I too will be indifferent to what happens on earth, like everyone else. But that takes time, and there are so many voices not yet hushed. A distant hubbub from professors and criminologists and private investigators and journalists. They say you die three times. The first time for me was when my heart stopped beating beneath his hands by the lake, and the second was when what was left of me was lowered into the ground in front of Ivan and Raksha at Bromma Church. The third time will be the last time my name is spoken on earth. And so I am waiting for it to happen. I wish all the voices would hush soon. I don't like hearing my name. It crawls like insects in the place where my heart once was.

If I were to say who did it, would the voices be silent then? I don't think they would, and no-one would believe me anyway. And it is so difficult to distinguish the light from the dark, and even harder when you are alone and time has ceased to exist, and space too. So I make some attempt to understand the difference. I have always confused love with insanity, heaven with death. I believed for a long time that the drugs came from the powers on high as compensation for my little brother. I don't believe that anymore. My little brother and I were blind alleys. Eskil walked into the river when we were children and didn't come back and, much later, I walked out into the immensity of the night to find him. Although sometimes I think I only entered the darkness because I had nowhere else to go. Maybe I knew I would never find Eskil there, in those endless labyrinthine nights, but it didn't matter, the other world was already closed to me. In any event, our family line stops here. That last part isn't really true, our family carries on with Valle and Solveig, even though they don't know where they come from. Sometimes I see Raksha's features in them both, appearing in their faces like a fleeting ripple in the water.

It is strange that I fantasise so much about Solveig. I don't know her and I never have. All I have is those two hours on the maternity ward when she was a tiny bundle of warmth in my arms. But it is easier to think about her than to think about Valle, because I never did her any harm. I kept her safe by making sure she would never need to be with me. For Solveig I did the only thing I could have done, even if Shane could never forgive me for it.

We were in the forest. The sky above was criss-crossed with black branches and I told myself they were lightning cracks leading into another world, and this was the world I was travelling towards now. "Here I am, God," I whispered. "Help me God, whoever you are."

In the forest, where we were now, the only sound was of flowing water, water running everywhere, out of the lake, the sky, the treetops. I had that vague reeling sensation of watching everything from above, as if I were fluttering up there like a trembling angel. All the laws of vision had collapsed, only fragments of broken images through which I viewed the world: his back in a light-coloured anorak, the back of a large head, pale freckles covering hands that squeezed a girl's neck on the grass. I saw the girl resting there against the earth's dark membrane, and it looked as though the ground would swallow up both him and her as he clung on to her like a giant beetle. "I only want to be close to you," he whispered to her, and I heard it even though I was floating some distance above. I wasn't dead yet, but I was already floating. And then my hearing slipped away. I was glad, now we were moving within a sphere of complete silence. Without the sense of hearing, it was easier to see, as if the world became clearer and the colours more intense. I thought maybe the world had been filled with water because everything was happening so slowly now, time slackened its pace, the gods held their breath.

*

Out of the treetops and flowers flew demonic images, all of them featuring me. I didn't want them. Grimy frames of film, momentarily lit up and immediately extinguished, they dropped from the trees like blazing flypapers and I shut my eyes, but the images seemed to be projected inside me and the whole of me was alight with these pictures. There I was, sitting with Valle at my breast, looking down at him. There was Nanna cycling through the first snowfall, before the filmstrip snapped and the forest came back. And now the man entered the girl lying on the ground, me, into the dark opening between her legs, his fingers interlaced like a corset around her throat. A storm howled inside me and maybe that was why it was so silent outside. I saw a single butterfly teetering in the black grass beside the girl and the man. It must have been a snow butterfly because it was white. Were there such things as snow butterflies? Did butterflies exist? Did the world still exist?

Yes, it did exist. A string of vertebrae existed, large square pearls that formed a backbone that had once been mine and now was broken. There were sinews that had severed. There was my windpipe, through which air still passed back and forth, used air pushed up out of his lungs and down into mine, a mixture of carbon dioxide and fire and hunger for blood. And these lungs that had been mine were filled with black blood. A body existed, on top of mine, and it was so heavy it didn't feel human; but human it was, this was what humans did, and this body crushed me against the earth and soon I would be earth myself, dark and cold and full of writhing worms. I had wished for something that would pin me down to the earth, a weight, a rope pulled tight across my wrists and ankles, something that eventually would hold me down and stop me. But this was not what I had wished for. Not this forest, not this hunter. Or maybe this was exactly what I had been waiting for all the time. Perhaps I had always hoped for a way out of the world, the black hole suddenly opening to devour me.

I saw a cloud collide with the crown of a tree and be rent apart. I saw the pupil in an eye quiver like a compass needle. I saw the little tree that Raksha had planted by the river when I was born and it must have been uprooted in a winter storm, for now it was hanging upside down between heaven and earth. I saw its branches growing downwards to the black soil while its roots reached up for the light of the sky. The branches made me think of veins in a placenta or arteries filled with a deadly black liquid as they grasped for the depths of the earth. I saw Valle in front of me. He was crawling around by himself at Sergels Torg wearing only a little nappy and high above hovered a bird of prey, waiting for the square to empty of people. And I saw myself, sitting at a table at Burger King, waiting for a dealer, as the huge bird dived out of the sky and took off again with my child in its claws.

And when the air abruptly returned, I dropped back down to earth, to the perspective of the slithering ground. I saw the world from below, I saw the sky skating from one fixed point to another and the light falling in golden shafts through the treetops. He had loosened his grip for a second and the world had come back with its choppy, broken light, the butterflies and the drooping dandelions, and then he took out a knife and it gleamed like a little mirror in his hand. A butcher's knife or a hunting knife and I am sure only the Devil would have answered me if I had knelt in prayer. Just before death, when fear and pain are overwhelming, the quarry is stunned. As it is for animals, so it is for human beings. When it is too late to defend yourself and futile to try in any case, the terror and despair transmute into a gentle anaesthetic fluid that unfurls like a vapour through the bloodstream.

Once, in the beginning, it had been like that with the drugs as well. When the bubbling brown liquid shot through my veins, something happened, something akin to this last moment of my fate at his hands, when everything suddenly stilled and I stopped fighting back. As the bewitching fluid swept through me, so vanished the feeling of being inferior and unworthy, of being nothing more than a piece of vermin to be eliminated. Because when this world holds no hope, your body goes numb and fear vanishes, as if the fear that has preyed upon you, day and night, was never there, and you float in the moment before death, like a patch of sky.

Even though I was so young and at the very start of something, I had always had the powerful sense of being at an end, standing right by a precipice I was about to slide off. Rubbish, feeble, weak and useless, a Friday-afternoon dud amidst that mass of fifties' girls the world didn't need, who would disappear one day without trace, missed by no-one.

We were on our way through the trees and the last stretch of the path was narrow and stony before the forest finally opened out to a lake lying before us like a shining mirror. Did I think it was my grave, that I would die in the water?

The rain was falling on the trees and the trees had stood there for a hundred years or more, their realm a slow and silent one. And they saw everything happening in the human world but couldn't intervene. If I had begged to stay and make one last call in that telephone box just before we reached the silver lake, I would have stood inside the misty panes of glass, a large black receiver in my hand, with choking, rattling breaths, and snot and saliva and tears dribbling from my nose and mouth, and fear like an icy claw around my spine. And if the rings had suddenly been interrupted by Raksha picking up in Svart-viksvägen – according to the map still no more than a few kilometres away, in reality separated from me by a whole universe – I would probably just have dropped the receiver and left it dangling at my feet with her voice calling out. For what would I say? "Mamma, Mamma, I don't know where I am."

A long time ago, when I was still a child and was making a call to Raksha from a telephone box outside the church by the river, my hand clamped around the large black receiver as if it were life itself, it seemed as though I would never breathe again if I didn't hear her voice. Raksha's heartbeat was in that telephone receiver and nowhere else. She had left and gone to Stockholm and Ivan was sinking deeper into his loneliness on the kitchen sofa. And all I had was her voice living in the telegraph wires running under the ground all the way down from Stockholm, where she was clattering along in a metro carriage far below the city in which she and I would later live without Ivan. But this time it was too late. This time there was no way out. The raindrops running down the windows were as large as globs of spittle sliding down the streaked glass with unnatural restraint until they hit the ground and disintegrated.

The summer was this formidable, fusty space, so vast and monstrous, and these trees so primeval where they stood, their crowns heavy with water. In the car he sat absolutely still, as though he was listening to a voice within him that drowned out the radio music, and he had no thought that I might dash into the forest and flee. The headlights illuminated the world of rain around us and everything apart from the two of us was swallowed up by the creeping mist: the city, the people and the future that no longer concerned me. He switched the radio off and all that could be heard was the slow sweep of the wind-screen wipers and the warm sound of the engine and in some places the sky was so low the trees seemed to disappear into the clouds. Long ago I had tried to stretch my hands up to touch Eskil in heaven.

And I could still have run away, *run, run, my heart,* into the forest like an animal. A faint sun glimmered through the rain-laden trees and it was still possible. He opened the car door and looked at me and when he turned to the forest his gaze was impenetrable. I could have disappeared into the trees if I had run now. But the thing is, even now I had nowhere to go. The forest would have come to an end and I would be standing at the side of the road and he would come driving past again and pick me up and drive me back here, to the banks of the silver lake and the slurry pit. So I remained sitting in the car, which was gleaming white against the faint brownish light settling on the landscape in the heavy summer rain.

"Come on," he said.

And even if time hadn't run out and even if there had been someone to call, Raksha or Shane or an angel, I still wouldn't have had anything to say. For what could I have said now that I hadn't managed to say before? Perhaps the reason I was already at the end, too soon, far too soon, on this muddy road at the edge of an unknown forest, was because I had no words for who I was and what I had come from. Inside me was voiceless silence, above me only a bare, defenceless sky and beneath me the earth's unrelenting gravity, pulling me down.

"Mamma, Mamma, I don't know where I am."

"Is that you?"

"Yes, I think it's me."

"Whereabouts are you?"

"In the forest."

"You have to tell me where you are so I can help you."

"I can't."

"Why not?"

"I don't know where I am, I told you."

"What can you see around you?"

"Rain and huge black trees. Ancient trees. A lake a bit further away. And birds screeching. No signs . . ."

"You mustn't hang up now."

"I only wanted to hear your voice. That was all I wanted."

A few weeks later they found me. It was a woman out with her dog at daybreak. On the shore below Haga Palace there was a white suitcase containing parts of me. Later that summer they found another suitcase by a cliff at Hägersten right beside the motorway. They transferred the contents to a room of death, and this was all there was left of me. A pelvis with genitals and uterus cut out. Two arms, a femur, a calf and two breasts, but no head. And since the head was missing, cause of death could not be ascertained; in other words, they couldn't rule out the possibility that, like Snow White, I had been poisoned by an apple or had choked on my own collar.

Nobody missed me at first. Valle and Solveig were too young and too far away, placed somewhere along the length of Sweden. Shane had disappeared and that I didn't turn up at the local authority office when I should have done was nothing unusual. That was how it used to be. I came and went, and sometimes I went to ground and would be gone for months. For a long time, Ivan thought that was it, I was somewhere under the city, in the metro system or the culverts beneath one of the big mental hospitals. Ivan always had his theories and at the end of that first summer he began to search for me. He never believed it was me in those suitcases.

I could have told the police right from the start how it would end. I could have said straightaway that there was no point in bringing anyone in for questioning, the perpetrator would deny everything, that is what they do. I could have told them he would say that he had never met me, that he had never been to the desolate street that runs like a gaping wound over the Brunkeberg ridge. The guilty deny death with such force they end up believing themselves. And my life is no longer a legal concern; the statute of limitation expired ages ago. What sort of concern am I then? No concern whatsoever, presumably. I died, that was all.

We were at the edge of a lake in a primordial forest somewhere beyond the city. I had gone with him in the way I always went with people. Because I needed the money, because I had a mission that went on day and night and there was nothing outside that mission. "To be free," as Nanna would say. "To punish myself," as people who thought they knew a thing or two would say. What should I be punished for? They never said. I had followed him like a dog.

In some other time, something about him might have caused me to back off when we were on Herkulesgatan, to shut the car door and walk away. In some other time, I might have said to Nanna and the rest of them that they should beware of him, but that time was as distant as Nanna was now. Of course, you learn to pick up the signs on the street, it is pure instinct, but in the end you can't even bother about signals any more. Signs such as the sky suddenly opening over the Brunkeberg ridge, letting unbridled light flood in, violet-yellow and ominous. Or the harsh strident squawks of the white bird screeching from the roof of the bank headquarters. Or the cloven-hoofed beat of the music streaming out of the car radio. He said it was Mozart, but it sounded like death. The silence hung over him like a cold smoke, the Arctic sea smoke that rises out of the water at dawn, and now I know the same silence enshrouds a grave.

I had arranged to meet him on Herkulesgatan. I was still

wearing the wristband and joggers they had given me in the hospital and I had on my fox-fur boa and a pair of red shoes. I was clearly of this world, but it felt as though I was dead. I had brushed with death so many times, I had stopped being afraid and for some reason I had been flung back into the world of the living once again. He stepped out of the shadows.

"Come on," he said.

We drove out of the city. When I turned and looked out of the back window, the road we left behind us was a sinking nothingness of mire and decay and the buildings were toppling into the abyss.

The forest we were in was inundated with brown water; I remember thinking the lake must have burst its banks because all around was the sound of running water. No, it wasn't nature weeping. Not even I was weeping. And the ground had a strange undertow, as if invisible hands were snatching at me from the underworld and globs of dank saliva dripped out of his mouth onto my face.

The mellow sunshine that had lingered in the air made every movement restrained and slow, almost suspended.

"I only want to be close to you," he whispered, and I laughed, because it was so unexpected, such a childish thing to say, almost comical, and I wasn't afraid anymore and all the pain from the hurt before was gone now. I laughed, and I heard the hard, metallic noise I made, and I wanted to say something, but when I tried, earth dribbled out of my mouth, a turbid, greyish fluid, a mixture of sludge and slime and decaying leaves. And there was no sound, no words, just those lumps of graveyard soil and something white, a grainy, rancid liquid with the stench of truffle. He gave my head a quick, hard twist and from the side a sliver of sky reflected in my eyes. Sky, against my will. But what was my will, in truth? I had wanted to be free, light as a gossamer, but it didn't work. I had one hand reaching for the firmament and one hand scrabbling in the mud. And in the heavens, night was falling now. Pink clouds, slightly frayed and fuzzy, clung to planet earth's great membrane. How could there be such beauty in heaven and such horror on earth? Where do you run to when you have nowhere to go?

"I only want to be close to you," he whispered, over and over. It sounded like a sermon and I laughed again, louder this time, and I don't think he liked people laughing, especially not girls, because then darkness came, as if someone had thrown a blanket over the sun, a dreadful howling blackness, and I was falling through an immense void. In the passage of an instant and a thousand years. I prayed for an angel to come, but there was no angel. I hoped this wasn't the end, but it was.

One day nothing about my story will matter anymore, not even to me. One day all of us will be part of the thin black layer of earth that covers this planet, amongst all those who died in bygone times. The human body is so easily damaged, its substance mere fluids and chemical compounds. Our bodies give us a place in time, and time is a form for evil, a vessel for dark encounters. Though sometimes I think brightness is worse; there were instants entirely without shadow and yet Shane and I couldn't sustain them. Like the moment Valle soars into the sky in his baby swing and Shane and I watch him whizzing away and hurtling back towards us. And now I have so much time, I see that all along he looks at me with eyes full of openness and trust, and those eyes still have faith in me.

Raksha's birthday came and went in June, soon after I turned twenty-four. Even though I didn't keep in touch at any other time, I always rang Raksha on her birthday, so she began to count the days. Two days passed, then ten, and suddenly it was three weeks. It was a time when nights were never more than twilight, when daylight lingered all night long, summer nights when dawn was just a breath on the horizon, a softly glimmering veil. Did Raksha realise I was dead, that I was no longer anywhere in this world? Was she aware that what had once been part of her was swimming in liquefied remains? Did she feel relief when they discovered the suitcases, a kind of wild release, something forbidden that went through her head like a flake of ash from a night-time fire? *At last it's over, there's nothing left to grieve. Not Eskil, not her.*

When I was seven I was given a baby brother. It was the best thing I ever had from Raksha and Ivan. We used to keep him in a laundry basket and transfer him from room to room, like a tiny candle that we had to keep alight. But a few days before my twelfth birthday he drowned in the river.

Raksha and I are in the same situation. We should have every opportunity to understand one another, and yet we never do. Then again, perhaps we did understand one another, but we didn't like what we understood. If I turned up at her house now, she might ask, like she used to ask, "Surely you've missed me a teeny bit, my silly little girl?" And she would be right, because I always longed to be with Raksha, even though I was hurt by her every time I came close. Later she would whisper, in her stifled, guilty little voice:

"You know I'm always so clumsy. I lose everything and miss what's important."

"Yes, I know."

"I even lost my beautiful babies."

"That makes two of us, Raksha," I could say at that point, since it was true, even if nobody cared about the truth any-more; but there is a certain kind of misery you cannot share, at least not with the one who bore you.

It is an archaic landscape swept by cold, harsh winds; it looks modern but it is ancient. A cluster of islands surrounded by motionless seawater beneath a naked sky. A patchwork of faded facades in yellow and pink with modern buildings made of black steel and glass. Bank headquarters, shopping malls and multi-storey car parks have a futuristic look, but age-old thoughts fill people's minds, ponderous, inalterable; there are victims, there are perpetrators, there are witnesses, and they all peer down at the ground. The well-heeled live in the centre, as they always have. And the lifeblood of this city circulates along Herkulesgatan and from there to the banks, the money moves in and out of the state, and the architecture framing all of this is raw and cold. Some are doomed to failure, others destined to advance, a certain few will rise above the rest; and you can see the early signs, children defined from the start. A secret watermark or a caste mark glowing under the skin on a child's brow. And in this city there is also someone who has been stalking me for quite some time, or chasing someone like me, a girl who no longer cares what happens to her. Let us call him the huntsman.

Imagine this scenario, and a city on the go, cars and people and the pulse of the future beating in everything; the future is all around us for now, sweeping like a mighty motorway or river through the landscape. We believe it will take us with it, but to think about the future is to yearn for death, and there will always be someone left behind on the riverbank, abandoned in the mud and mire. Now imagine a chequered public square in the middle of the city and a few metres from this chessboard I stand and wait.

We had met a few days earlier, on one of the many evenings I spent on Herkulesgatan, and he had said:

"I'm going to show you something. I think you'll like it."

There were very few things I liked in the world and I found it hard to imagine that this would be one of them, but I didn't say it.

"What if I don't want anything anymore?" I said.

"Well, you'll get it anyway. Sometimes you get things you never knew you wanted."

The light emitted from the streetlamp above was like electric rain, static and grey. Streetlamps had been installed here a while ago, to get rid of the dealers; I kicked the lampposts every time I walked past them and sometimes they went out and night would descend again over the street and I could move about without feeling pursued by the glare. He had been fingering something in his coat pocket, a small silver packet that he produced. It was straight morphine, he said, and it was absorbed by the heart. A pure sensation of fire and gemstone; and I had always thought that drugs were like being on fire without burning yourself, falling without hurting yourself. In the end, of course, you did hurt yourself, sooner or later you fell through the world before people's eyes, but the sensation is what I am trying to describe. And so it was. We fell together, Shane and I. The tragedy of falling is that it takes such a bloody long time, because you can't help resisting, even though you long for it to end. I really wanted something to defeat me, but it didn't, the will to live kept on ticking inside me like a terrible eternity clock. That is how you end up waiting for a hunter.

"I think I know what you want," he had said. "I think I can give it to you."

He was talking about death, but I didn't realise at the time, I thought we were talking about something else; I was thinking about my mission, unable to think beyond that. It is liberating to have a purpose, the only thing to fill your being, a form to inhabit, like a prayer. He was thinking about death. A secret desire forcing through him like a surge of water.

"OK," I said.

Because the hunger tore through my blood vessels. A storm raging within me, drowning out everything else. I only hoped he wasn't one who liked to talk. It was always the same story anyway, and I didn't want any more stories, I wanted reality to be an open, bleeding wound. That was why I had loved Shane; he never lied to me.

There he sat in his car with the passenger door open, waiting for me, without saying anything, not even looking at me. As if we already knew one another, as if we had an agreement. He didn't seem particularly eager; he was neither angry nor drunk. He wasn't dark either, and by that I mean the kind of darkness that encases certain people. He sat still as a statue behind the wheel and if I hadn't seen his lips move I would have thought the voice came from inside me.

"Are you coming then?"

"How did you find me?" I asked Shane once, right at the beginning.

"I was always looking for you," he said. "I just didn't believe you existed until I found you."

I didn't believe it either, that the person I became with him existed. The girl who was afraid of nothing, whose laugh made people turn in the street. It was as though life finally began when I met Shane.

Before we had Valle, I thought that if I was still going to perish, I wanted it to be with Shane; I believed that if I died it wouldn't matter, because I would die with him. I had pictured our dead bodies so many times, it was as real as if it had already happened; we were lying side by side on the floor in an empty apartment, lips black, eyes open. That, for me, was death, and the image no longer scared me. I never stopped to think we **might not be together when death came.**

The only thing that moved inside the car was a single black-and-white photograph vibrating in the draught from the blower on the dashboard. The photo was of an old woman whose eyes were so pale it looked as though the iris and pupil had burned out. It was hot and stuffy in the car and the seats were scorching against my thighs from the sun; there was the smell of Little Trees air freshener and sheet metal. When death comes, it comes quietly. No tattooed lilies, no Devil's footprints. You climb into a car as you have done a thousand times before, with no thought for the past or the future, no notion that fate has prepared something special for you. And yet you know. When you sift through your memories afterwards, you understand it all, you see everything as if through cold, clear water. You see his entire soul, the solitary beast of prey resting beneath the wavering sun before it springs. You see the gods hold their breath.

"Are you coming then?"

It was just like the deadly disease that would take all my friends later on. We saw it make a grab for us like the hand of darkness on Herkulesgatan, but we all thought we could deal with it. No prayers could relieve that sickness; it interfered with love at the very moment two bodies became one pulsing eye. But by the time all that happened, I was long gone.

*

Nanna and I used to sit on the bridge over Kungsgatan and watch the cars speeding past below us. We always sat up high and looked down on the streets and it gave us a sense of eternity, at least for me. Up there we were untouchable, no-one could get at us while we sat like old thieves or angels watching over people's lives below us. We could face anything as long as we were able to sit there together raised aloft above everything else. We laughed at the old men and the young boys, we laughed at the people who were agitated, or sentimental, or furious, we laughed at the people shouting for their mother or for God as they passed.

"Working the streets is like being in a bloody church service," Nanna said.

Her words always set us free, like her high, brittle laughter.

I think I should say a few words about my childhood, but it feels so remote, as if it happened to someone else, and I don't know which parts of it I ought to include. A lot of what happened much later seems more relevant, such as becoming a mother myself, or dying. First of all, you are condemned to being a child, like being in prison, and then one day you come out and find you are responsible for your own life. What difference do the experiences you have had actually make? I think of Raksha's silky hands, the freckles that looked as though they were sprinkled over her skin, and her face as she lay sunbathing, half asleep, by the riverbank. I remember how the whole of her was soft as sand, the smell of her hair, the sound of her voice.

If I was going to relate anything, it would be the time I went to the hospital when I was seven and held Eskil for the first time. He still smelled strongly of the sea and ancient times and he had a little tube in his nose because it was difficult for him to breathe. I sat motionless for hours gazing at this strange being that had just come out of Raksha. I could tell you about everything else that Raksha gave me, without her knowing she had given me anything at all. How she cut everyone's hair by the river; how they came up to us with their bad, unkempt hairdos and left like new people, revitalised. They always had something to drink while they waited their turn and some-times, when there was a crowd of people waiting, there was a party and Raksha would put her scissors away and join the party instead. But it didn't matter, because most of them were out of work and they came back the next day. The best days were when she said I could miss school and stay at home with her and we would sit at the kitchen table all morning in our nightclothes. Ivan would have left ages ago, long before we woke, and Raksha would play her first game of solitaire and smoke her first cigarette, humming along to the radio, slightly hungover, while the cigarette smoke curled gently up to the ceiling. I never thought about her not working, apart from the haircuts that came and went periodically. Sometimes the place was full of people waiting, sometimes no-one came for months.

"Blow me a smoke ring, Mamma!"

I used to ask her to make a smoke ring for me and after she had done one, I begged her to blow another into the first one. To me the whole smoke-ring thing was a miracle. When I grew up, I would smoke like her, I thought.

Here, in the wind, you can hear the voices of all those of us who disappeared against our will. I hear the echo of our loneliness, I hear shouts and prayers and children crying. I hear the ugly sound of blood spattering on walls, of locks turning in morgues. I feel thousands of hands slowly burrowing into children's bodies and staying there forever. I hear screams from the slaughterhouses, from children's bedrooms, from unmarked graves.

It sounds as though many would have wanted to stay a little longer and catch the remaining light, but the question of will is complicated, an illusion for the most part. It is so easy to confuse liberty with living out a dream, with intensity, isolation, death. You might as well get used to the idea that life is not going to be the way you want it to be, that one day you too will sell a bit of yourself. Maybe not your cunt, but most certainly your soul, at the perfume counter in Åhléns or as director of some television company or president of a youth group. So I believe it was determined from the beginning of time, or at least from the moment I emerged from Raksha's womb one night at the end of the fifties, that I would meet this hunter in the forest.

Death has its advantages as well. When you are dead it doesn't matter if you are a loser and can't pay your bills. When you are dead everyone thinks they were fond of you and they forget your bad points. They miss you and want you to come back, but nobody considers what would happen if you actually did, if, for example, you were sitting on Raksha's sofa one day when she surfaced from one of her tablet-induced dreams.

"Hello, dearest Raksha."

"Heavens! Is it you?"

"Yes, I'm here again."

"I had a horrible dream about you."

"I know, but death let me go. I fought and kicked so hard I was let loose."

"My God. It was a dreadful dream. Some pill dreams are truly awful. Well, what shall we do now?"

"I don't know. I only just arrived. Tell me what's been happening here instead."

"Um, well . . . my new doctor's absolutely fantastic, he's a bit like Jesus, he lets me have as many tablets as I like. So today, to give you an example, I had nothing but sleeping pills for lunch."

"I can see why you're happy then . . . And Ivan must have been here?"

"Ugh, that creep . . ."

"But weren't you glad he was here? I got the impression you were."

"Yeah, maybe. But now he's gone again. Just as well."

And then she would look around, puzzled and slightly embarrassed, and we would sit there, and all the difficulty between us, everything that had been temporarily erased by death, would be back: that she wasn't the mother I had needed and I wasn't the daughter she had wished for. But who gets everything they wish for?

I was so young when it began, no longer a child, but not yet a woman. I don't know if I ever did become a woman, but one day I couldn't stand normality anymore and that was when I crossed over to the other side. I stood in a rain of broken glass with my first syringe in my hand and if I could, I would tell you how beautiful it was, as if all things were suddenly illuminated from within. A glass wall that was soundlessly smashed and gave access to the world.

One day you find something that makes you free, genuinely free, like a child who is lost in the forest and brought up by wolves and never finds her way back to what there was before or can never even remember that there was something else before. You chance upon it after an eternal night in Vitabergsparken and after that you are no longer afraid of anything, of the night, of strangers, of dying. Later the fear will return and take everything, pushing you to the ground, but for now you are just a beached mermaid, reclining on the bonnet of a car.

A girl with amber eyes and soft hair, who later will turn out to be Nanna, has helped me tighten a blood-red belt around my upper arm. Her hands are pale as her eyes, an artificial, washed-out bluishness, but her nails are a glittering apricot. Her hair makes her look like a fairy-tale creature; I find out eventually she hides behind it when she is afraid, and it is so fair it merges into grey.

*

My heart is beating as though it is perched on the outside of my body, and this is a point of no return, I know. Whatever I may say later, I know. At the hour of the star, you know. You know because this is precisely what you want, never to return to what there was before, to your old self. The last thing you want is to be yourself and it is so simple, simple as a heartbeat, a small silver packet over a flame and the smell of vinegar pervading the room, like no other smell I have ever known. A musty, lifeless sea, the inside of a coffin, of a shell. And when the needle hits a vein and the bubbly brown fluid mixes with blood, I vomit straight out into the room and my genitals contract like a jellyfish. We go out to the street, Nanna and I, and it is like walking through water or waist-high snow or pure love, and all at once I am lying on the bonnet of a car with Nanna's hand in mine, looking up at the cold, naked sky and never has it been so close, floating above me and yet inside me too. Someone kisses my neck, not Nanna, she has disappeared. Someone finds my mouth in the streetlamp's silver light, and that is where the world begins, where it opens up. I still have not made love to anyone, never been naked with anyone, never kissed anyone, but after this I am a virgin no longer. An angel, fantastic, unknown, intoxicated, has raped me and dragged my soul out into the bitter cold of space, never to give it back.

It is not that I am instantly addicted that first time, because I am not. I wake up in a room filled with sunlight after many hours of deep sleep, a strange, looping sleep, and my body is relaxed and soft and normal and the others have left, all except Nanna, who is asleep beneath the open window in her underpants and vest. My Detroit sweatshirt is in a heap on the floor, covered in puke of a faintly pinkish colour. Next to me on the sofa is a white feather, which I put in my handbag when I leave. When I walk home along Drottningholmsvägen it is different, reduced somehow, narrower, greyer, despite the bright sunshine. A lifeless world. No birds, no trees; there they stand, and yet they are not there. A silent blue sky, bottomless, faceless.

It is silent in the apartment; gently quivering shafts of sunlight extend like pillars into the kitchen. I snuggle down behind Raksha and fall asleep at once. It always used to be me waiting for Raksha, and now at night Raksha waits for me. She sits at the kitchen table until dawn when she gives up and goes to bed. Days pass, and everything is as it always has been, and one morning on my way to school I take a detour past the metro, and next time I look at my watch it is too late to go to school. Because now that I know about it, I can't ignore the fact there is somewhere else, an outside, with more room, or a truer place, a paradise that can rise up inside me at any moment, and it is the place I have been looking for all this time. There is no compulsion, it is not that I am forced to return, but I want to go back and let the angel take me again, harder.

Nanna opens the door when I ring the bell, her skin white as snow, her eyes paler than ice under the sunglasses. Later, people will say we are so alike, though she is fair and I am dark.

"Hello, Boomerang. I knew you'd come back."

"Did you know I'd come today?"

"I thought it might take a bit longer. But I hoped it would be today."

*

39

Something dropped out of heaven for me when I met Nanna. It was made of silver and gave off the scent of ash and ammonia, and I imagined, when I sat next to her and once again she tightened the thin belt around my arm, that what was flowing into me had travelled far, perhaps for many years, to reach me, and it was given to me because I had waited so long for Eskil. The water took him, and therefore it took Raksha too, and as compensation I was entitled to this feeling, unlike anything I had ever known before. And I was given Nanna, who was so much older than I was and had no fear of anything at all. It is a state of holiness, the little blue flame and the dark liquid coursing through the blood, the heartbeats drawing me into another world. And there, in the magic spell, I finally meet Eskil. He is walking towards me out of nowhere, like a fairy tale. Wearing the same bright-red bobble hat he always wore, he is just as small and beautiful. His lips are black, but his eyes are clear and full of light, as if he were alive. He stands quite still by my side, looking up at me. And I had forgotten how little he was, just over a metre tall. His hand as dainty as a flower.

"Are you very angry, Inni?"

"Why would I be angry?"

"Because I drowned. I thought you were angry because I didn't listen to you."

You think you are always going to be angry, but then one day, you are not angry any longer. One day you are not anything.

"I'm not angry. But Raksha's missed you so much, she nearly drowned herself. But no-one's angry with you."

His eyes move from side to side, as if he is following

something in the sky behind me, a bird or a plane, though there is nothing there. When I touch him he is cold.

"I don't believe that. I think she's angry."

"Raksha's just annoyed with herself for being such a fool. I am as well."

He still smells so good, he still smells of Eskil, with a hint of sour milk, and washing powder. His eyes are darker than I remember and I daren't touch him again even though he is standing right beside me, so close I can hear his breathing. I love his tiny breaths.

"I should have come for you, but I didn't know how to find you," I say when he doesn't reply.

"It doesn't matter. I'm fine now. Everything's fine."

"Are you sure?"

"Yes, I don't need anything here."

"Not even me?"

"I wanted to stay with you, but that wasn't to be. They took me. And I don't think I'm allowed to miss anyone here."

"Who took you?"

I reach out a hand to him, but, as I do, he disappears.

People peer up at the sky and I wonder what everyone is looking for. Everyone except Raksha, who sits at the window, staring down at her hands. They are old now, veiny and yellow, and her nails look like claws. I love those hands so much, I want to touch them. She sits all day doing crosswords, when she is not lying in the bath, staring at the cracks in the ceiling. Out in the street she keeps her eyes firmly on the ground, terrified of meeting another human gaze. She is so lovely, sitting there alone, waiting for death, and I never tire of looking at her. A little while ago I heard her singing to herself. Sometimes I think Raksha looks exactly as she did when I was young, just a few sizes smaller; she has shrunk, as old people do over time. She still colours her hair a crazy shade of reddish orange. Although she never goes out, she is very careful the silver doesn't show, not even as an outline at her temples.

One day somebody telephoned and asked for me. It was a man, he didn't introduce himself and I assumed it could be someone from before, who still had my number.

"She can't come to the phone at the moment," Raksha said.

"Why not?"

"Because she's dead," Raksha said, and hung up.

When it rang again, she pulled the cable out of the socket.

VERTIGO

It was the summer I had disappeared. Every afternoon Raksha sat on the sofa, looking at the grey square that was the television, afraid there would be something about me in there, if she switched it on. No other news item that summer held the same fascination as the one about my body in white suitcases. The television was her closest friend, but now she felt as though the people inside the set were looking at her accusingly. They were glancing in her direction, even when they weren't talking about me, and she wanted to go up to them and explain. But what would she say? *That thing without a head in a suitcase is my child . . . Those pieces of flesh floating in liquefied corpse, that's my little squirrel . . .*

I couldn't understand how this Raksha, sitting and looking out of the window with a cigarette burning in the ashtray in front of her, could be the same Raksha I had always waited for when I was a child, the person who once had filled my field of vision and embodied my entire world. They had the same name, the same face, but they weren't remotely similar. She had smoked before too, but usually she would take a few hard drags, brisk, strained, almost slapdash, before crumpling the cigarette into the ashtray. And she had always been in a hurry. Now she was sitting perfectly still, watching the smoke rise to the ceiling, where it slowly dispersed into nothing. Smoke is time getting away from her, and it can't be stopped.

Whilst the city outside Raksha's window was a river surging ahead without her, her own time stood still. The flies collected on the flypapers and the rubbish remained in the bin. She would sit for the whole day, looking at the hoarding over the front of the building on the opposite side of the street. If it hadn't been there, she would have been able to see the sky, but what she saw instead was a photograph of a view and a woman in a swimsuit running across a beach. Raksha looked tired, but her heart was beating so violently, it was visible against her dress. I would have liked to lay my hand there, to calm it. The advertising vista on the wall opposite was all there was, now that she could no longer watch the television. And she didn't read anything from her water-damaged books the way she always had before. The type mingled with the wood pulp and slipped away from her, despite the magnifying glass at her side. Around her the world was silent, but inside her it roared.

She hadn't told anyone I had been found. But one day she sat down next to the telephone. It transmitted its electrical signals and she heard Ivan's voice, scratchy and defensive, and after so many years, it brought back a whole world from the past, of the wild thrill of night and the sound of cranes drifting around in the twilight and of deep unhappiness, and she asked him if they'd had any snow, even though it was the middle of summer. And when it went quiet, she heard the sound of a football match in the background. He won't want to be disturbed right now, she thought, and she wouldn't wish to disturb a living soul, not even herself. She wanted to drowse in the bath and let the days drain away until there were none left.

She had no idea how she would phrase it, what words she would use to describe the sky crashing down on her, cascading to the ground. Words were intangible, empty and strangely weightless, at once too forceful and too meagre. So she said:

"Are you watching football?"

He mumbled something that might have been a yes.

"That'll make you happy. But now I'm afraid I have to make you sad."

"You've always done that," Ivan said, but his voice was unsure now, slightly less rasping, as though really he knew what was coming, but hung on nevertheless to the world of before, which in a few seconds' time would be gone forever.

*

It was the first time he had heard her voice for many years and it still had the same effect on him, made him hollow with anger. He was quiet and so was she, both of them waiting for her to say something, and in the silence he was suddenly struck by the smell of her, as distinctly as if it came flowing out of the receiver into the room. She smelled acrid and intoxicating, a little like glue, a scent that had once made him drive for miles through the night, just to experience it again. Instinctively he held the receiver away from his head to avoid what was coming next, to escape the intrusive odour. In his heart of hearts, he knew what she was going to say. There was a newspaper on the table in front of him. For the last few days my body had been drowning in printers' ink on newspaper billboards and now here was Raksha's breathless voice in the receiver after all these years. The photographs of my face hadn't been published yet, and there was no name, but the articles about my mutilated body had fluttered briefly past Ivan's life, as news does, like bats in the night, scary and entertaining in equal measure. I was the sort of news that drew a circle of light around the reader and inside that circle there was warmth and sharing, where you were safe. Outside the circle was where we were, the shadows.

Raksha groped her way through the syntax of death, listening to his breathing. The syntax of death was this: if she said it was a tragedy, so painful was the understatement, she found it difficult to breathe. She found it hard to breathe all the time. And if she said she wanted to die, it just sounded like something you say when you've made a spectacle of yourself at a party. Besides, she had been saying she wanted to die for as long as she could remember. Was it only her speech that was devoid of content, or was it the whole world? Where was the language to describe what had happened? Sylvia was the only person she had seen since and she had said nothing to her.

"Why aren't you saying anything, Raksha?" I had whispered to her a few days earlier, while they were sitting on Sylvia's balcony in the sunshine, smoking. Maybe she was trying, maybe she intended to tell her, but no words would come out.

"You're going to need someone now, you stubborn old mule," I said outright, into nowhere. It sounded like a tiny gust of air passing through, that was all, and I realised the only person she wanted to speak to was Ivan, there was no-one else who could understand, despite the distance. And now she did speak.

"She always rings on my birthday," Raksha said. "She rings and asks what I'd like and I always say I just want to have her back . . . So I thought . . . So then I thought, well . . . There's so much time to think . . . Actually, for the last few years I've just been waiting . . . I really wish I could have called you about something else, now that I'm finally ringing after all this time . . ."

Ivan hadn't seen me since I was fifteen; for him I was still the skinny kid that Raksha had taken away with her on the train so long ago. At first I went down to see him, but then I stopped going. Raksha had written asking for help on all those occasions she was at her wits' end. The last time was when Shane and I lost Valle. Ivan had never answered her letters, but he had read them – they were gathered together in his bedside table, envelopes opened. I had been Raksha's child from the start and for as long as I can remember, I had reached out for her.

It wasn't that I was afraid of Ivan, it was more that he never seemed to see his children properly. We belonged to a different species, our voices on a frequency he didn't catch. All he saw was Raksha, and her very spirit made him furious. At that time, by the river, he and Raksha and their love devoured everything around them. Us as well.

When we did eventually leave, Ivan stood on the platform smoking a farewell cigarette, talking to a woman in a red coat who was also there to wave someone off. Or did he already know her? Ivan made friends with people so easily, always starting conversations with strangers; maybe we were the ones who never got to know him. He had offered her a cigarette and now they were standing there looking up at me hanging out of the window. Raksha hid in her seat in the compartment. As the train started to move, he said something.

"What did you say?" I shouted into the high-pitched whine in the overhead lines caused by the train's motion.

"Never trust anyone."

"Can't I trust you?"

"Least of all me."

Raksha twisted the telephone cord round her fingers and dried her eyes with the hem of her dress. She wasn't weeping, but water poured out of her eyes all day long now, streaming silently out of her. She wavered and started again. She was ashamed of waiting far too long before calling him. She had told the police there was only her, there was no-one else, and that was true, really, there had always only been her. And after that she couldn't bring herself to telephone. Days had passed, as she sat with the receiver in her hand, listening to the single tone. On paper they were still married, they hadn't even got around to sorting that out. But what difference did an official certificate make after such a long time? She felt as though she must be unhinged now, to be pestering him with what had happened to her daughter. I came from her, both Eskil and I came from her. The fault was hers. But be that as it may, she carried on.

"You've always said you don't have children anymore. So I was ringing . . . I was just ringing to say, I don't either now."

When he didn't say anything, she continued.

"Someone cut her up into pieces – how should I put this? Her head's gone. Maybe you read about it in the paper? And her holy of holies too."

She didn't say anything else after that, and nor did he. White and perspiring, she looked as though she had just spewed her guts onto the floor in front of her.

They sat in silence, each listening to the breathing of the other and the faint sound you used to hear in those days of voices on telephone lines from every part of the world. I imagined there might have been a woman in Poland making a similar call to a Polish man. Far away, Ivan sounded short of breath, he took a few sharp gasps, but he wasn't crying. Not that she could hear, at any rate. After a while she lit a cigarette and took a couple of draws so deep I thought I heard it crackling in her lungs. Then she said, "Ivan are you still there?" When he still said nothing, she whispered, "Goodbye then, my friend." And she gently replaced the receiver on her side of the world.

It was the blue hour, the hour when the sun and the moon met and the first tremulous night-time light and vestiges of day-light merged like magical waters and swathed the world in a quivering violet phosphorescence, when everything grew soft and nebulous and all the outlines and shadows melted away. For a while we just sat there and he didn't look at me. His hands were resting on the wheel, his eyes focussed on the world before us, and at this point he hadn't turned the engine off. What were we waiting for?

There was a smell of old leather and detergent, as if he had recently scoured the entire interior of the car. A single child seat in the back, a teddy bear lying in a ray of sunlight on the seat. A rosary of beads on the rear-view mirror hanging in blue droplets in front of me. Afterwards I assumed he wanted to give me one last chance to escape. I had the feeling he could see straight into my soul, past all that had already been and beyond what was to come. And there was no way to elude those eyes, the black ink pouring out of the pupils under the ponderous vault of his eyelids. There was no way to avoid what was coming. And now with a purr the car started to move. The gentle stirring of a beast of prey.

We drove through a mellow green landscape, groves of young birch trees, derelict houses and a sky so low, it looked as though we were driving into it. On the dashboard there was a photograph of a woman; his mother, I guessed. He wanted her to watch him all the time, I thought, whatever he was doing, and now there was something he wanted to show her.

"It's beautiful here," he said.

"Do you think so?"

"Yes."

"OK."

"Don't you see it?"

"No."

The world seemed to be heavy with rain, a world of rain in which the green appeared in sharper focus, a world immersed in water. Treetops softly dappled with chlorophyll. Asphalt dark with rain. Bloodstained shadows of animals now dead. Badgers and birds. That was what I saw.

"I don't like nature," I said.

"Why not?"

"You can't hide."

"What do you want to hide from?"

"The massive glare."

"You're so cute, you don't need to hide."

It was quiet for a moment, and then he offered me a small silver packet, the packet I was hoping for, the packet I was here for, a packet that glittered in the dim light. I took it and opened the stiff foil and searched for matches. And as always when the smell of burnt metal and vinegar rose above the little flame, my groin tightened in a spasm, a showering of silver inside me and the gentle touch of an embrace from within, and the rest of the world faded away, as if it had never existed. I pushed the needle into the crook of my arm and there was no rush, it was a long time since there had been, but it worked the same spell on me every time, my heart shuddered and grew still and I fell through the layers of time until I was floating inside a womb. The sensation of the needle pressing into my blue-blotched skin, the buzz of electricity deep inside me. I closed my eyes and leaned my head backwards, and it was like following a wood nymph into the forest, hypnotised by her dancing backwards, and suddenly realising, when she finally turns and you have no idea how to find your way out in the dark, that her back is an open wound of rotting black.

And that was the thing. I never really wanted to give up heroin. Not properly, not even for Valle and Solveig's sake. It is the kind of insight that makes you weightless, the knowledge that there is something greater than all love.

I had told him what it would cost, two hundred and fifty kronor, and we had agreed I would go with him. The price had dropped of late, and I had sunk deeper into the mire and slime that existed beneath the city, below the earth and asphalt where the filth gathered, in the underground sewers and metro bunkers where people lived like ghosts.

We drove along the motorway and I don't know if it was the rain or time running out like sand in an hourglass, but in certain places where the landscape opened out after miles of pine forest, you could actually see that the world was round, that it curved in an arc along the rim of matchstick-sized trees in the distance.

"Where are we going?"

"Wait and see."

"I can't see anything."

"Sleep for a while if you like."

He drove with his eyes on the rain-soaked road as if in a trance, concentrating on something within himself that had nothing to do with me. I don't know why, but suddenly I was telling him about Eskil. I had never told anyone else, not even Shane.

When I was a child, you could see the glint of fish like lightning silver slivers across the surface of the river, before they disappeared again to become striated shadows on the bottom. You could see beavers in broad daylight. Eskil and I used to spy on people bathing in the river. From the trees we could see the beavers swimming right next to them and they never even noticed. Small glistening heads with black peppercorn eyes watching humans at play. Only we saw the beavers, from the drooping trees on the riverbank, where we sat all day in summer. Only we two had enough time to notice them. The river had its source further upcountry and after it had passed the power station it sped on, its currents flowing like electricity, like menacing hands snatching at us. At least that was how it was in our day. It is no-one's fault if a child disappears in circumstances such as these; it is the forces of nature and the particular weight someone has in water. And if that person can't swim, he sinks like an object, like stones and shells and the black sand on the river bed.

"Poor kid," he said, sitting next to me in the car, and I didn't know if he meant me or Eskil. His gaze was wide open, no shades, no animosity, and for a moment he was my confidant, almost my friend. But it wasn't a friend I needed, it was a cure, for what I was. I needed something to believe in, I needed a miracle; but it was too late for miracles.

Perhaps he too was searching for a miracle, a release, a kind of absolution. He needed someone like me, had been looking for a girl for whom the world held no more fear; apart from fear of love and of salvation. "Poor kid," he said again. For that second, I don't believe that he had any intention of hurting me. But when I turned and looked out of the back window, there was no asphalt, no verge, no road signs, just the motorway fracturing behind us and collapsing into giant craters in the ground, as if there had never been a road that we had travelled along.

He drove slowly through the rain, as though he didn't quite know where we were heading; but he did know, he had studied the maps, he knew everything there was to know about the forests around here, he had marked the slurry pit by the thousand-year-old silver lake on his map. They existed in those days, dark holes where you could dump things you wanted to disappear, really disappear, a pool of glossy pink corrosive sludge over which the metallic green blowflies gathered in summer. Maybe they don't exist anymore, those slurry pits, maybe they belonged to a different age, I don't know for sure. Anyhow, he slowed down more and more, as if he wanted to drag out the moment as long as possible, it was so precious. It was precious for me as well, considering it was my last. I thought of Valle's hands when he had just been born, how they opened and closed like jellyfish, how he seemed to be making a grab for life with those tiny fingers, making a grab for us. And then later, when his little hand sought mine at night. I thought of Shane, of him singing to me in his cracked voice when I couldn't sleep. I thought of Solveig, of never knowing her.

I should have done the same with Valle as I did with Solveig. Not tried to soften the harsh core of coercion in the gentle voices of the social workers, the fate that had already been sealed for us, that had only to be fulfilled before my eyes. But from the start I said I wanted them to take Solveig, and so it was. I had gone to the social services office, still a few months to go, but Solveig was already moving in there in her weight-lessness, and her heart was beating, they said. As it should, they said. It would soon be a bit cramped in there, and she would come out, but for the time being she was mine alone.

"Do you understand what permanent means?" the person in charge asked. "You won't be able to get the child back if you change your mind."

"I'm not going to change my mind."

"And you won't be able to see it again."

"I don't want to see her again. She'll be better off without me."

But now the huge black trees on either side were making everything dark. Massive treetops heavy with rain bowing down as if in prayer and the landscape closing around us like a cage. It was too late for prayers. But then I've already said that, haven't I?

I have never prayed to God. "You ought to," said those people at Storsjön who had taken over the care of my child. What should I pray for? To get Valle back? In the face of their unimpeachable, ingratiating prayers, I would stand no chance of keeping him. And how do they know it isn't Satan they are invoking when they pray, those self-righteous tossers? I have nothing to say to God, and nor to anyone else for that matter.

All I know is that I got into that car on that twilit night at the beginning of June.

"I've been waiting for you," he said in a low voice, without looking at me, as we drove past the airport. It was the first thing he had said since we set off.

"Have you?"

How could he know who I was? I, just one of all the anonymous people who lived by night in this city, like a bat on the world's flip side. And no-one here knew who I was, I scarcely did myself, and I never said my name. I said I was called John Wayne or Snow White, I said I was on my way home after an awful storm. And in a way that was true. It was just that there had never been any home before the storm. I had taken off long ago to find something, and what that was I could no longer remember. Now he turned to me and his eyes were so intense, I was forced to look away.

"Maybe you've been waiting for me too?"

I hadn't, and I said so.

"What have you been waiting for then, my little friend?"

"I've been waiting for a miracle."

He smiled. It looked as though someone pulled sharply on a string at the corner of his mouth, and made his smile vanish in an instant.

"Which one?"

"Which what?"

"Which miracle have you been waiting for? Not Jesus?"

The nature of a miracle was such that you couldn't imagine it in advance. All you knew was that it would change your entire existence forever. How could he not know that?

"Why would I have been waiting for you?" I asked instead, since I didn't want to talk about miracles.

"I don't know. I just thought you might because I've been waiting for someone like you."

"Like me?"

"I've been waiting for someone who's not afraid of anything, who doesn't fear for her life anymore."

It was so long since I had felt fear, but I did then, a trickle of dry ice along my spine.

I looked out of the streaked window at the rain falling from the heavens and I saw the trees bending over the road. It was June, it was the month for disappearing, the month for being found in pieces, the month for losing your head, and your tongue and your genitals. Solveig's eyes followed me wherever I went, and whenever I closed my eyes I saw hers, quite still and clear, gazing at me from eternity. We drove through a tunnel of rain and flowers and trees and the world was now just one single room, one single chamber, a grave and a coffin, a wall of trees that would all soon be dead. But first I was the one about to die.

I told myself I had always been heading towards this moment, always travelling on this dark, muddy road leading out of the city, and when I turned and looked out of the window at the back, I saw the road cave in and disappear behind us. No road ahead of me and no road back. It was something I had thought so many times, without understanding how many roads still existed then. But now they were gone, irrevocably, and for a second I was struck by a sensation of freedom, a wave breaking over me, dazzling green and cold. It was Eskil's wave, the cold, clear river water, and I realised that what happened to me no longer mattered to anybody on earth, and it didn't matter to me either. I said, "Do with me what you will."

A solitary bird seemed to fall out of the sky, swooping over the silver lake a little further away. And I supposed death was merely being outside time, being outside a human body in which time could be measured. That was the only way to comprehend it; death, and time. But now there was nothing else to comprehend, at least not for me.

All beasts of prey leave the entrails behind, and the hunter did too. My intestines were left on the little brown mudflat in the forest. They soon disappeared, dragged away by a vixen whose young were in a den nearby. It is the natural order of things; we are brought into being in order to be given up to death. Perhaps it is our only function? To become food for the animals. The birds came back later to eat what was left of me. My last remains taken by a flock of jackdaws, pieces of smooth pink flesh ascending with the jackdaws from the shore to the firmament.

It is very fortunate birds exist, and maggots, and decay. If we corpses didn't lie in the earth and decompose, we would be piled to the sky, high-rise blocks and towers of the deceased. I often reflect on how many we are, those of us who have already taken our leave, so infinitely many more than you who are left. And yet we can't do anything to you. You can do what you want with us, say what you want, throw black earth on top of us and tell whatever stories you like. No-one can check the facts with us, that is what is so nice about the dead. A perfect friend, someone who never argues, and we never change, we stay the same as we have always been, frozen in tableaux. A person is forgotten in two generations; that is the extent of human memory.

*

And what else did he say in the car, driving along the main road to an unknown forest? He said he was a hunter, that he had a job as a butcher, that he was an architect. Or did he say he was a judge? It doesn't matter now; this was a world I didn't want to live in anyway.

It was the summer I had disappeared. Raksha went into the bathroom, ran a bath and slid straight into the water. Why had she said, "Goodbye, my friend," to Ivan? They had never been friends. They had loved like a pair of dogs, but they had never liked one another. Raksha had never had any friends at all, she had me and Eskil when we were little and that had been enough for her; and after us she had nothing whatsoever, that at least was true. Pills were her best friends, unimaginably wonderful friends, meek and docile, never troublesome. Sylvia in the apartment below was always trying to worm her way in. She would follow Raksha's every response with another question, her prying eyes on everything, wandering the whole time, and she would spot anything left on show. Sometimes Raksha would drape a cloth over the books on the shelf, because she thought they revealed too much about her. Otherwise Sylvia would stand there, staring at the titles, as if it was a bloody library.

She looked down at her body lying in the bath, flabby and ugly, with skin sagging from her stomach in a way it hadn't before, maybe because the only things she ate now were sleeping tablets. She had done everything she could to survive in this world. And for this? Now she felt as though she had known all along what was in store for her, seen the shadows gathering in her life, and that was why she had wanted to leave for good. She had seen a great sorrow ahead of us a long time ago, but it was like a cloud that was constantly moving, and she and

Ivan were so happy tearing around, they ran straight into it. At heart, she had known from the beginning that both Eskil and I were too much of a miracle to be real, she had known she had only received us in order to lose us, in a gruesome game that entertained the gods after a night of roister. And now we had been transformed in her head into the impossible dreams we had actually always been, intangible, elusive soap-bubble versions. In her dreams we were in our winter cardigans, crying and looking at her, and when she tried to reach for us, we simply disappeared. That was what she learned from the dreams, that she mustn't touch us, or we would instantly slide away and dissolve. So she didn't touch us, she just gazed at us for as long as she could. That way she could prolong the dreams. And every time she woke, it was night-time in the world; and in the end she had got it right. She had instinctively wanted to shield herself from what was to come, and she hadn't been able to. She had been made to stay in the world, as if governed by a dictator, and there was no-one to tell that she had been right all along.

She had always been afraid of falling stars, had never wished for anything more than those children we were. She had tried to keep her demons to herself, without success. In a way, Raksha had been dead for a long time. She had lain in the bottom of a coffin and looked up at the little assembled company, which was me, standing there weeping, hoping she would rise again like a second Jesus. She dipped under the hot water in the bath, and the world was soundless and filled with warmth, like the unfailingly soft light in the realm of her pills. She had called Ivan and now she would never need to ascend to the real world again. In the apartment beyond, the telephone rang, a sharp, exhorting sound, but under the warm water she didn't hear it. It rang a few times and then it stopped.

Every time she took a bath, she stayed in the tub long after she had let the water out. The little eddy that swirled round the plughole as the last of the water poured out was her life, a tiny spiral of her life's light draining rapidly away, to no purpose. When the telephone rang again, she heard it, jumped out of the bath and answered it, naked. It was Ivan.

"You're back."

"Yes."

"I was in the bath."

"Ah."

He was silent. And so was she. She twisted the telephone cord round her finger so hard it hurt. She thought she must have been the one who had rung him, and he was annoyed.

"Did you have something on your mind, Ivan?"

"I wouldn't have rung if I hadn't."

He sounded angry again.

"I can talk for a bit if you like. I just need to put something on. Will you wait a second?"

"Yes."

She hurried out into the hall and pulled on a coat at random, a winter coat, and then she sat down, perspiring, the receiver in her hand, hair dripping, the ornate belt pulled tight round her waist, waiting for him to say something. And that was how it went on. He rang again that evening and early the following morning and soon she started to wait for his calls, and when he didn't ring, her stomach began to ache, but then the shrill noise suddenly filled the apartment again. And there they would sit, saying nothing. She grew accustomed to his silence; indeed she knew it well from before. They had often been at home together, in silence; they could go months without saying anything.

In the course of those telephone calls she sometimes heard birds chirping in the background, he must have opened the window, and she remembered the sky, how low it always was by the river, how it had been everywhere; whilst in the city there were just brief glimpses here and there, and she had always missed it. Sometimes she heard the television in the background and she switched hers on to see what he was watching, and they sat there, watching together. When he was with her she wasn't scared of the television, and anyway he only watched football matches. Ivan's breathing was right beside her in the receiver, and just as it had once filled her life, it was filling it again; she couldn't understand how this could happen so fast, when she had coped without it for so many years. Whenever there was a goal, he cheered. It made her happy; inside she was cheering too. And when the match was over, they quickly switched off, before the news started. Then they sat in silence once more, and nights came and went; she had stopped waiting for him to say anything, it would feel almost absurd if he suddenly began to speak. In the evenings she fell asleep with the receiver in her hand and when she woke the room was light and the sound of birdsong flowed through the receiver, such a loud sound, so close, as if the birds were singing inside her. She didn't dare think about the cost of these telephone calls.

*

Raksha no longer tore the pages out of her calendar; she hadn't done this since the day the police called. She was living outside time, perhaps she had been for a while, but now she didn't know if it was day or night, summer or winter, war or peace, if she was young and still waiting for life to begin, or if she was already lying under the earth; and it was comforting not to know. She had heard someone say on the radio, during a programme about death, that if time and space no longer existed, there could be no pain. Evil needed time and space to operate.

It was early morning and she had slept with the receiver in her hand as she had every night for the last week, and now she woke to a single tone beeping in her ear. She immediately replaced it in the cradle and waited for him to ring back. And when he did, a few minutes later, she said:

"Do you want to come and see me, Ivan?"

"No," came the quick reply, in his rasping, gravelly voice.

Then she had hung up and heard nothing more, but the next morning he was at her door with his suitcase. She had just woken up and opened the door wearing a T-shirt, bare-legged. She had slept all night because he hadn't rung, and before she fell asleep she had wept at her own stupidity, and now she thought he was Sylvia, wanting to borrow something for some stupid baking.

Ivan had taken the night train, he mumbled, standing outside Raksha's door, looking down at the fossil-streaked stone floor, to find out more and do what he could. He didn't trust the police and he couldn't afford to stay in a hotel. What he might want or could afford made no difference to her, she could see he was furious with himself for coming and furious with her. There were no words for love and none for death. So she walked into his arms and held him and listened to his old, angry heart beating inside him. After a while he shoved her away, of course he did, he brushed her aside like a clinging cat and stared at her with the ice-blue eyes that had always made her feel so unclean and loathsome. But now they had no effect on her. She had seen what she needed to see, found out what she needed to find out. They drank coffee together, maintaining their silence; he took a shower and had something to eat, and then they put the television on, the afternoon repeats. He could do what he wanted as far as she was concerned, as long as he didn't leave now. And when all the programmes were over, he came to her. They went into the bedroom together. She lowered herself cautiously onto him and they sank into the blackness together.

He couldn't do what he did before, but it didn't matter. This was something different, as if they were two very elderly people. He was shaking, and she wished she could help him be still. In the dark room it was as though they had just come into being; when she looked down at her skin it was shimmering, her clothes had slipped off her body unnoticed, the flabbiness had disappeared and the broken rawness that was usually there was also gone. Gently he stroked the scar under the elastic in her pants, and perhaps he was thinking of us, of Eskil and me. It was still red after all those years, a botched stitching job, and sometimes it still hurt, a tight, burning sensation. Raksha gasped with fear when he touched her, her breathing quick as a bird's and halting, afraid he would suddenly get up and leave and take the night train back and never be in contact again. But he stayed where he was, and she found no malice in his eyes. When he bent and kissed her on the scar, I looked away. This was not for me. This was their hour on earth.

Raksha and Ivan came flying in from nowhere and became a family, a sudden constellation which was as arbitrary and haphazard as a newborn cloud in the sky, as transient and momentary as a flock of birds rising up as one, doomed to scatter in the wind.

The years by the river when Raksha and Ivan stayed up all night and Raksha woke me with her hearty laugh, I would lie in my bed listening to their voices drifting through the apartment in gentle loops. Suddenly Eskil was there next to my bed, with his bright little halo of hair.

"May I come in with you, Inni?"

I used to carry him back to his bed after he had fallen asleep, there wasn't much room in mine, but after a while he would be back. I never understood how he could know where I was when he was asleep, but he did, and in the end I let him stay. He lay curled up in the crook of my arm, while the winter storms roared outside the window. Sometimes I would get up and follow the low voices in the room next door. A tune was playing on the gramophone in the sitting room, a violet trail.

They were often up all night, Raksha and Ivan. Then they slept for half the day. It wasn't possible for anyone else to reach inside their world; they had sealed themselves off in something that was made of the two of them alone. In this first light of day they look so young, like they did before, and when I look at them now I see how short their lives have been, how little they know. Although deep furrows are already drawn across their faces. I look at my parents, Raksha and Ivan, gently dancing in the dawn, cheek to cheek.

"Mamma?"

She turns, pulling slightly out of his embrace. She has been crying, black streaks under her eyes making her look like a raccoon. And she has been drinking; how would she survive otherwise? Then she turns away and they carry on dancing, locked into the paradise and the hell they constitute for one another. They are alone in the world, those two, no relatives, no family, at any rate none that came home to us. When I watch them now, I don't know whether it is before or after what happened by the river. But when I go back into our room, Eskil's bed is no longer over by the window, so it must already have happened. The wardrobe has been emptied of his clothes.

They knew no other way of living, Raksha and Ivan, and without alcohol they were lost. It was as if the sun rose inside them every time they brought out their bottles. A sun that turned black in the end, after a few days or weeks of drinking, but even so, they would never have coped without that black light. It was a hunger I inherited from them.

You could say we lost Eskil because of Raksha and Ivan's drinking, that they were bewitched by each other and the light they found in alcohol. But it could also be said that higher powers were out for Eskil, and they would keep on trying until they succeeded. He was always hurting himself, stumbling over stones and doorsteps from an early age and hurting himself, falling out of trees and off rocks. As though a large hand in the heavens was making a grab for him. We had warnings, premonitions, but we didn't listen.

NIGHT

I would like to have my head back, I miss it. They always dispose of the head first, to eliminate the horror of looking a dead person in the eye. It is the gaze they want to get rid of; that is why they kill, to extinguish the light in the eyes, the stranger staring out from a foreign land. The head often ends up in a rubbish chute or a skip. Not mine; mine disappears into the slurry pit with the pink surface, sinking slowly to the bottom; and as it descends, my hair opens out like a little parachute over my head. No-one ever comes to find it. The thick, frothy liquid dissolves my face first, and then the rest. I would rather have been a skeleton in a secondary school somewhere, sitting there empty-eyed, an earthly representative of the dead.

We had reached the lake now, where the road came to an end at the edge of the forest. It felt as though we had been driving forever along the muddy road that receded behind us. When the engine stopped we sat in silence, surveying the lake's silvery sheen; a solitary black bird, soaring and dipping over the inky surface, the world's last bird. As if we were both waiting for something to happen, for the sound of icy wing beats from an ageing angel who would eventually come to my aid. But I was tired of angels, tired of hoping for rescue and deliverance; no-one could help me now. This was the place for my death, this was my great window to eternity, my trapdoor out of this world. I longed for the sound of the coffin lid closing above me, for everything finally silenced. No birds, no sky, no light, no escape.

"May I smoke in here?" I asked; after all, we were only sitting and waiting. I wondered what we were waiting for; perhaps for the courage to take my life, the courage I didn't possess myself. I imagined he might be afraid too, as I was. What was I doing in this terrible forest by this awful lake?

"Of course, smoke if you need to," he said, opening a small ashtray on the dashboard.

"Would you like one?"

I wasn't in the habit of offering; I was usually asking for cigarettes, even when I already had some, to avoid ever being without.

"No," he said. "I detest cigarettes and alcohol. They're disgusting."

He was funny, he had forgotten he was talking to a junkie.

"OK," I said, and lit what would be my last cigarette. And for one last time the little flame flared in front of me, the innermost cone of blue, the smell of sulphur stinging in my nose, the smoke spreading quickly in the small car.

"Go on, smoke, my child," he said.

I smoked, and I looked at the woman's photograph on the dashboard. She was waiting too, just as we were, and I hoped Eskil was waiting for me in some place a bit like a heaven. She had an age-old look in her eyes, as though she were viewing us from the perspective of eternity, her gaze stern, introspective, her eyes so pale they seemed inhuman.

"Who's that?" I asked eventually, for something to say, and because she was staring at us. My hands were shaking as I held the cigarette, there was a twitch in my eyelid; I think my fear excited him.

"She's part of my work."

"I assumed it was your mother," I said, to win time; suddenly I wanted more time. For what? What would I do with more time? Time was up, and that was what I had wanted; that there would be no more time.

"I don't have a mother," he said, getting out of the car.

I didn't know where I was going, but I knew I couldn't take anything with me. Whatever happened, my bag would be left behind in this world. I wished I could take it with me. At least the photos of Valle. Though I do have those inside me, etched behind my eyelids. I don't have eyelids any longer, but you know what I mean. I travel light. With little baggage.

"So how did your mother die?" I asked. He flinched, as if I had hit him. Now I think he hated that word more than anything else.

"Have I said she's dead?"

"You just said you don't have a mother."

He gave me a quick look, as though checking to see who I was. Maybe there had been so many girls in his car, he couldn't be sure it was actually me. Did it matter that it was me? I keep thinking I was chosen, but it might have been pure chance, or that thing called fate.

"Just because you've lost someone doesn't mean that person's dead," he said, and we spoke no more. There was nothing left to say.

I needed to prolong time, even though I wanted it to be over quickly, but it was the end itself that frightened me. I was afraid I would suddenly start running and be caught in his hands like a rat; I was afraid that something inside me would flare up, a will, an eagerness, a pulse for survival. I knew what he meant. No-one had died, but I had lost Raksha long ago. She had continued to be there, but I was no longer her child.

"I can't be your mamma any longer."

"Why?"

"There's nothing left."

"But I'm still here."

"It's not enough, Inni."

In hindsight I thought that possibly we were alike, the hunter and I; the same inner lassitude, the same way of sitting and waiting, of not running, not trying to repress what we had inside us, the precipice, the huge destructive force within a person, unseen, but relentlessly dragging her down. But I didn't say that then. Instead I asked:

"May I smoke another cigarette?"

"No. Shall we go?"

It wasn't a question, it was instruction for what was going to happen next. So I got out of the car and I left my bag on the seat; I hesitated for a second to pick it up, but I knew I wasn't going to need it anymore. It had been a present from Shane on my twenty-third birthday. That felt like a thousand years ago. I wondered what the shadow walking behind me would do with it, the grubby little white bag in which I kept everything I possessed. I wondered what he would do with me. I wondered what he would do with what was left of me.

Here at the edge of the thousand-year-old lake there was no longer a world; there was nothing, nothing to indicate that humans had ever existed on earth, only the smell of still water and the mist drawing in like smoke over the landscape. "Here I am, Mamma," I whispered. Perhaps I was already dead, I thought. Maybe he had already chased me along the road, caught me and dragged me into the ditch, pinned me down and strangled me and cut me up and buried me. Maybe I had already bolted into the shadow that was death, like a roe deer darting between car headlights, incapable of leaving the flickering light, doomed to run into it and be crushed by the coachwork. Maybe I was already travelling outside time, outside the world, even though I was still here, by this ancient lake; I didn't know if I was alive or if I was something else, I didn't know if I was earth or blood or nothing. I hoped that Raksha wouldn't have to see what was left of me. *It won't be me, Raksha.* I wished I could miss out the end. But the end came, and I was there.

And across time and the forest and all the forest's sounds, I can hear Shane's voice. It is close and soft and runs through me like gently flowing water.

"The difficult thing is giving someone something she's never had before."

"Why is that difficult?"

"Because, no matter how beautiful it is, if she's never seen beauty before, she won't recognise it."

"But I was never ever afraid with you, Shane."

He is silent for a moment, before his voice returns.

"But I was always afraid when I was with you. Don't you understand?"

"I'll always be afraid of myself when I'm around you," Shane said, burying his face in my dirty sweater. Darkness had fallen while we were making love, something we were not going to do anymore, and bats with outstretched wings flitted between the night-time trees above. As I lay there watching the tiny shadows skimming like flakes of ash in the air, I knew that if I could do it all one more time, I would choose Shane, again and again and again. For those moments of total closeness, when he was searching for veins along my arm while I was trembling; when I saw the fleeting shift of Valle's face in his; when I was standing by the window about to jump and he shook me, to make me understand that I was hurting him. The giddiness and tenderness when he pulled me in and we collapsed under the window and Shane wept so much I feared he would break. We were horrified by what we aroused in each other, but it was greater than anything else we knew, and only love can scare off evil. But since love is invisible, we have to believe in it, and that was what was hard for me, because I have never believed in anything. Not in love. Not in anything. But, I do believe in death, that death is the end. That is what I hope, that everything really does end here.

When Shane and I got married we stole the flowers from a grave on the way to the church. A bunch of white lilies that he held to his heart as we stood before the altar. Behind it hovered Mary with her baby Jesus. There had been occasions when we had slept in this church, on the floor between the pews, but now we were here to get married, even though neither of us believed in eternity. It was not that sort of age and we were not that sort of people. I looked at him standing next to me in an old suit we had picked up from a charity shop that morning; it was slightly too big and it smelled of mothballs and eau-de-Cologne. He looked happy and fearful, his hair still a little wet – we had bathed on Norr Mälarstrand on the way there – and it looked as though he had just been born. And Shane and I promised to love one another for better or worse. It wasn't difficult to make the promise; I still woke every morning and thought he was the most beautiful person in the world. The difficulty was keeping promises. But that is the very thing about marriage, that the ceremony erases the past and you get the chance to start again. We had never stopped loving one another, hadn't even achieved that; we had tried, but not succeeded. The tears that had filled Shane's eyes when we stood before the higher powers never spilled again. It was an eternity since either of us had wept. When despair grows so deep, weeping is no longer an option. The church bells rang and when we went out into the sunshine the brightness blinded us and we walked in different directions down the steps, I to the right and he to the left, and we had gone several metres before we realised the other wasn't there. I was contained within myself, unreachable, dazed by the strong sunlight, faint with a hollow, uneasy joy. I don't think we told anyone we were married, not even Nanna. We had no witnesses, no Valle, no confetti falling like rain when we came out of church; I don't even know if the marriage was registered anywhere. Nothing was ever real for us; we tried to imitate the rituals of real people, without succeeding. The worst thing is, I believe Shane truly loved me.

"Can't we do something crazy, something totally wrong?" I had said.

"What would that be then?"

"Get married . . ."

He laughed.

"How would that help?"

"I don't know, but we've been lonely for so long."

"Will we be less lonely?"

"We can be lonely together while we wait for a miracle."

"What kind of miracle?"

"I don't know. We'll just wait."

We never said to each other that we thought it would help us get Valle back, but that was the truth.

People always think it was Shane who dragged me down, but that is wrong, I was the depraved one, I was the one who wanted it all to be quick. It was undoubtedly the drugs that rescued me from love; I don't think we ever took as many as we did then, when we were newly-weds. At the end of the summer I discovered I was pregnant with Solveig. A small dark shadow growing in the landscape of doom inside me.

It was the first summer and my photograph was now in all the newspapers. I have always thought there is something unnerving about faces, they are so naked, it seems indecent. I would gladly show my fanny to all and sundry, but I don't want anyone to see my face, and especially not my eyes. Raksha and Ivan were sitting at the kitchen table, eating toast, looking out; it was the evening of their second day together. The stream of cars and people outside looked different to Raksha now she wasn't on her own, it had drawn nearer and she could see that all the coming and going out there was nothing to be afraid of. Women walking with heavy shopping bags, deep in thought. An occasional child tearing along the pavement; old people, alone, moving forward so slowly they seemed to be standing still. Like ships on the horizon in the Kattegat, seemingly motionless, but when after a while you looked again they had always shifted a little. There was nothing bad about the people out there.

Ivan said he had to go out into the city to search.

"For what?" she said, afraid he would disappear if he left the apartment, that his memory of her would be wiped in the fresh clear air outside. Instead of answering her question, he looked at her as if she were an idiot. As indeed she was, she couldn't but agree. She felt imprisoned by her fear. She had managed without him for years and now she had allowed herself to be taken captive again. If he left today she would jump out of the window. Certain things never wane and when she laid her head on Ivan's chest at night and listened to his breathing, there was nowhere else on earth she wanted to be. Not even the place where the sleeping tablets took her.

"But will you come home afterwards?"

"Home?"

His gaze always made her feel stupid. The coldness in it, as if he wished her dead. But if she were an idiot, then what was he doing here with her? Perhaps they each loved their own idiot, maybe that was what they had in common.

"I can come with you wherever you're going," she said, preparing herself for an even harsher gaze. But instead the hint of a shine crept into it, not much, but just enough for her to dare to fetch her handbag and put on her coat and stand in front of him, waiting.

"I might be able to help you," she said.

They were down by the waterside in the Haga district. The sun reflected on the water, and the air was soft, with only the faint scent of fire that typically drifted over the landscape at the end of summer. The sound of a plane flying overhead drowned out the noise of the traffic from the motorway. Ivan looked like a little general, scanning the water, back straight, on his guard. For long periods he ignored the fact that she was there, but sometimes they smoked a cigarette together or ate the polony sandwiches she had brought. They were still not speaking. There was nothing to say here either. Nor could they find anything. The landscape was closed, revealing nothing. The trees gave nothing away, they rustled their crowns, indifferent to everything apart from their eternal reaching for the sky. Or perhaps, like me, they had no voice.

"Mamma," I whispered, but no-one heard me.

Ivan had told Raksha he would be able to sense where the murderer was, that he would use his instinct, but actually he sensed nothing at all. And that place was like any other place, grass and sky and trees and the late-summer smell of still water lapping to and fro in the canal. They wandered about as though they were on a large abandoned map, narrow paths over there, clumps of trees over here, the palace there, but it didn't help, the landscape told them nothing. There was no trace of me or the hunter, apart from the flattened grass where the suitcase had lain. The smells were new, it had rained all summer, and nature, growing, striving, kept her secrets.

He came to her every night, defenceless, or bearing only the winged touch still there in his hands. It was as if they entered a room that didn't exist during the day, where they were as one, where there had never been any hostility between them, and every new day they went back down to Haga. She knew he didn't want to go there alone, but each day she was still afraid that he would leave her in the apartment. So she made sandwiches and put on her coat and then she sat down and waited. She would give anything not to be lonely again. It was an awful feeling. She missed the time when he hadn't been there, when she had been sufficient for herself.

At night as I was going to sleep – a long time ago, when I was still alive, when I was still breathing, in a toilet in Central Station or on somebody's floor – I used to picture our planet after we had all gone. The roads without cars, the cities emptied of people, and the stillness that would descend over the world when our species was no longer here, when the factories had fallen silent, when the columns of smoke that had risen out of them for two hundred years had disappeared, when there were no more planes in the sky. In my dreams I would fly over this gentle, hushed landscape and imagine that it wouldn't be long before plants would force their way through the asphalt and the motorways would disappear and in just a few hundred years all sign of human life would be erased. As I lay there I saw the vegetation growing, tendrils winding, trees slowly emerging from the windows of ancient buildings.

The shining gash of Herkulesgatan would be gone, the whole of the Brunkeberg ridge would have collapsed into the old shafts, as if it had never been. Department stores and government buildings and airports would be occupied by birds and the old bank headquarters would have caved in and huge trees would grow out of the ruins, stretching to the heavens. And the branches would be full of insects again, butterflies and dragonflies would return. The thought of everything that was our world vanishing one day calmed me. It wasn't only I who would perish, it was all of humankind.

Ivan told Raksha that something would come to them if they just waited, and time was an asset they both had. So they kept on, spending their days walking around the place where I had been found. The depression in the grass grew less obvious with every passing day. The pale brown patch disappeared, the colour came back and as the earth was touched by sunshine and rain, the grass imperceptibly pushed up. Sometimes it was so beautiful it made Raksha ache; when the sun set over the silhouettes of buildings on the far side of the bay and bathed Haga Palace and the rest of the world in a soft apricot light. She hadn't seen the world's beauty before now: the cobwebs glistening between the sodden tree-trunks, the clean smell of earth emanating from the ground at this time of year. She reflected on the wonder of them finally having a child again together. After all these years. The only thing was, the child herself had gone. In her mind's eye I would be a newborn baby lying in the earth, like a flower, cocooned in a chrysalis from which I would hatch, pure and pink and shiny. And the change was so gradual it was almost indiscernible: at first it had been the murderer they were searching for along the palace shore, but very slowly they changed their tack and it was me they began to seek, without saying it aloud. Neither of them had seen my dead body. They had seen me being born, but they hadn't seen me die.

It so happened that the hunter sought out that spot too, but always in the evening, and when evening came Ivan and Raksha would go home. The hunter walked around for a while, taking in the scene and its attendant smells, the earth and water, the strike of sulphur. There would soon be no trace of me left, the flattened, brown grass would be upright, the slight hollow made by the suitcase unnoticeable. He had wanted to leave some kind of sign, but it hadn't lasted. Just before the snow fell that first year he hung my bra from a nearby tree, but no-one saw it before it fell off and was buried in the snow, apart from a child who stood for a long time looking at it, until her father pulled her away.

"Look in the tree, Pappa, there's something in the tree."

It seemed to me there was a special luminosity about this place, but it might simply have been the glint on the water. Sometimes, in my mind, a hole opened up in the heavens above and an ethereal light trickled down through the layers of grey cloud and when it filtered between the trees it was like no other light. It was golden, a golden glow from another world.

Raksha and Ivan started going into the city in the mornings, they followed my footsteps, or what they thought were my footsteps, and they looked so lonely, standing on Herkulesgatan in the autumn rain, waiting. A man and a woman who appeared older than they actually were, paying avid attention to everything that was happening outside the bank headquarters. They didn't look like cops or social workers, they didn't look as though they were on drugs, they just stood there, in all their ordinariness and greyness, and scared off girls as well as punters. It might not have been a crime to stand as they did, hand in hand, staring in front of them, but a high-speed train coming down Herkulesgatan would have caused less of a stir. They looked as though they came from a different century: too still, too grey, as if preserved in ice. When I watched them it seemed as though a great divine hand were holding them down to the ground, but I haven't seen any gods here, so it must have been something else.

Sometimes they sat on the steps at Sergels Torg looking out across the giant chessboard and sometimes under the bare trees in Kungsträdgården. They didn't attract as much attention there as they did on Herkulesgatan.

"I love you, Ivan," Raksha said, as they waited in Kungsträdgården, sitting next to each other on a bench covered in bird droppings, each holding an ice-cream cornet. He didn't reply, but that didn't matter, he rarely did. She knew he would love her to his dying day, but as far as he was concerned, that was nobody's business but his own.

We had come from the river into the city, to the hospital. It was as if we had always been by that dark little riverbank with the black grains of sand, coarse sand with flecks of gold, as if until this moment our whole life had unfolded by the river and we had come out of that water with Eskil. When we emerged from an underwater land, reality was revealed to us for what it was, stark and merciless. We stood in the harsh light inside the hospital, under a naked, buzzing fluorescent lamp, illuminated and humiliated, and now when I look at us, I see our clothes are soiled with mud and seaweed and old river water. In this instant we became part of the world, ripped out of the great shadow we had dwelled in together, where we had been invisible to the rest of the world, free. Eskil was no longer one of us, he had been torn from our universe. He lay on a trolley and at last we stood beside him, the three of us; and Raksha leaned over him, wailing, her eyes burning with fear, and we could see that deep inside she was an animal, that behind her human form she was an animal. Everyone conceals something within them that others cannot see; the thought had always frightened me. This was what Raksha had hidden from me. And if I had been granted a single wish, it would have been for her to have Eskil back, and for him to have his Raksha back. I needed nothing for myself, I could forgo it all, if Raksha could only hold her child one last time. But that was not to be; this was the end, I knew.

*

I had known all along that this was going to happen, or so I thought. So why hadn't I said anything to Raksha? Why had I let him walk out into the river? Perhaps because, if it was to happen at all, it might as well happen straight away. Perhaps it was simply that my attention wandered for a moment; we had discovered a beaver's lodge by the huge underwater roots forcing their way down into the river from the trees growing up above, trees that were living off the river water, bowing their crowns over the river's brown membrane. I kept diving down to look at the little den, where I could see everything as clearly as if I held a magnifying glass in my hand. Beneath the surface time took on a different dimension; the water's inertia and gentle resistance slowed down earthly time and transformed it into underwater time, time that moved more slowly without the sounds from up above that could measure it out and give it definition. Nothing happened down there, nothing much at least; the shadow of a gleaming perch swimming past a little further on, particles descending in the serried rays of sunlight quivering through the water. What happened down there was slower than anything happening up on land. There was hardly any need to rise to the surface for air; when I was down there I didn't need oxygen, or food, or love. He was collecting driftwood and pebbles at the edge, as I had told him to, and I saw his shins and his flippered feet a few metres away where he was standing. But time moved erratically, for long periods it stood absolutely still and then in a trice it lurched forward. For then I couldn't see his shins; no time at all had passed, and yet they were gone. And here's the thing. Afterwards you see everything as it was, that is the essence of time, you see it precisely as it was, and it is as simple and clear as the sweet river water, as the stone on his grave, as the deep blue of the heavens arching over us when we lower him into the earth.

Raksha and Ivan were lying on a blanket in the sun, limp and drowsy with the heat, their legs entwined. It was a world of radiant light, and for a moment everything shuddered and swayed as it always did when you came up out of the river, before the world settled and regained its perspective and its rhythm.

"Has Eskil come back?" I shouted, as I hung on at the edge of the world, even though I could see they were alone. They rose slowly to their feet, I saw Raksha run, then fall and get up again. I dived back down to look for him. I guessed he might have swum out a little; he could almost swim, still doggy paddle, but nevertheless, he moved along with the back of his head under the water and just a little circle of his face above the surface. He was too scared to do proper strokes because they were so slow he thought he would sink; he didn't trust the slowness to keep him afloat, so he swam with his hands whirring like a propeller in front of him. And now he had swum off, despite me telling him not to, without asking, without taking me with him to keep an eye on those inept strokes that made him look like a puppy.

Raksha stands with her cold, mud-spattered child in her arms. In the hospital the clamour returns; there had been no sound at all by the river. None under the water, where the silence was total – that was why we were drawn there, Eskil and I, where the world was mute and iridescent green – and on this day no sound above the water's surface either. It wasn't far to the hospital and they put him on the back seat, but on the way there all the noise was absent again, we drove through a world that was utterly silent. And then we were standing outside the hospital room where he was lying dead. Or still alive, I thought, because I believed he was alive, even when I knew he was dead. Maybe everyone knew he was dead, apart from Raksha and me. Even after many years had passed, I still don't think she really understood. Perhaps you never do.

"He's in here," a nurse said, her hand on a door immediately next to us. It was as if the door had materialised in the wall the instant she touched it. Without a word Raksha backed away, unable to go into the room.

"I don't want to know," she whispered. And Ivan was somewhere else. As soon as we entered the building, he had gone. So that left me.

"You can come in if you'd like to," the nurse said.

Afterwards someone told us I shouldn't have gone in, but if I could do it again, I would keep going in. Because on the other side there was life, such as it really was. Eskil's half-naked body on the trolley, a heap of wet towels on the floor, spots of bright red blood, a group of adults pressing on his chest. It looked as though they were crushing him, as if they were trying to kill my little brother. Then I heard myself say: "It's not going to work, is it?" I don't know if anyone answered, I just said it straight into the room, to no-one in particular. Or to him, lying there in his bathing trunks, which were still wet. I think saying I knew it had all been in vain was a kind of self-protection. I still believed it might turn out OK, nothing was certain, Jesus had risen from the dead; but I didn't want to expose my trust, my hope against hope. The room spun, twisted full circle, but I was still sitting on the stool, I didn't fall off. It was like watching a film, so I just sat and watched. Since it was a film, it was all right. It was the only film I had of Eskil, and it had a bad ending. After a while somebody shouted that there was a child in the room. I didn't know if it was me or Eskil they meant. I just stayed on my stool. Everything was quiet for a few seconds when one of them standing next to him stopped pressing on his chest. Then another one took over. It was like sitting in front of a television set, and yet this was what reality was; it had been underlying everything, all the time. A crack had opened up that would never be closed; and through that crack there came no light, only total darkness. His hair was wet. What had happened to his flippers? That was foremost in my mind: who had taken Eskil's red flippers? It didn't matter now, because the time for play was finished, childhood was over. In any case, I had always hated being a child.

Enormous clouds are blowing in over the river and the children we once were are running faster and faster under the sky, and the sky is hurrying too, scudding past at speed. But the thought of running away from him never occurred to me; I ran a short distance, then I turned and waited for him to catch up. Every time I had a slight head start he was scared and shouted after me.

"Inni, wait!"

"Inni . . ."

He always thought I was going to run away from him or leave him somewhere. He didn't know I would have guarded him with my life, if only I had known what to guard him against. One night I woke to find him staring at me in the half-light of the room we shared by the river.

"Why aren't you asleep?" I asked, although actually I was too tired to speak and I wanted to return to my dream, where everything was soft and warm. But it wasn't like that for him. Sleep was a restless place and he didn't want to be there; in his dreams there was always something chasing him.

"I can't sleep 'cos I'm frightened, Inni."

"But I told you there's nothing to be afraid of. We're the only ones here."

"How do you know?"

"I just know."

*

We ran beside Raksha along the river, Eskil and I, one on each side of her. Raksha was the best thing we had. When she saw a falling star she shouted out, telling us we had to wish for something.

"Can't you see it? There . . . Now it's falling . . . Look!"

It was the huge comet everyone had been waiting for, the tail of light streaking across the sky, and anyone who didn't make a wish now would miss the moment for ever.

"But our wishes never come true," Eskil said. He didn't understand the importance of the comet, the fact that at this moment the whole world was watching it pass our planet, that it was close to being the end of our world. He looked at me doubtfully.

"Is that true?"

"If it's God's will."

"Is it God's will?"

"We'll have to see," I said.

We believe there is a connection between certain things, but maybe there isn't. Maybe it is all quite arbitrary. In any case, for Eskil it was too late; they told us later at the hospital, however long I tried, I would never have managed to blow enough air back into his tiny soul. *One breath, two breaths, three breaths* and then the wait with one hand on his scrawny chest, completely still, water and sand pouring out of his mouth, and if I just kept going he would soon come back. Since that time I have always had his little mouth against my ear, I still listen for those breaths that never come. The world beyond us both is a faraway murmur, never drawing nearer.

We had reached the end of the gravel road, travelled along it for so long, and around us time had slipped away, it no longer applied to us. We stopped at a farm; it didn't look as though anyone was living there, a grey film over everything, slurry tanks standing open like gaping mouths. It might have been a site he had discovered long before, or maybe he had studied plans of the area. It was as if this particular place had been expecting us. Located slightly off the map, where the rain poured in the wrong direction, up into the sky, a black, inverted rain, ascending against the force of gravity. Adjacent to the large house a barn like a naked skeleton, a few disused storage sheds, right beside the car a mound of dung I was about to step in. These parts were waterlogged, maybe that was why it had been abandoned. It has since occurred to me that this place, so very far in any direction from other houses and other people, had manifested itself there just for us. Wells with concrete covers and further away a pond with dry, blackened reeds round the edges. A tractor, a stone-pit, a solitary cat disappearing behind the house. He would soon be driving on and I still could have run, darted into the forest like an animal, but I didn't. For there was nowhere to run; and even if I did, I would come back here and he would be waiting for me. And why would I run? Why put off the inevitable? All stories end with death, and this one is no exception.

"Don't be afraid, sweetheart," he said, and started the engine. I said nothing, because I had nothing to say and this wasn't the right place, this wasn't where I was going to die. So we drove on. We continued until we reached a lake. I knew he was going to kill me, but I didn't run. Why? Because I had nowhere to go.

If he had told me then that I would never return to the city, that he would strangle me by that little stretch of muddy shore, would I have got out of the car and left? I hope so. But there was no-one waiting for me, I had nothing to hold dear and therefore nothing to fear; indifference was all I had. Dead or alive, it no longer mattered. I was already dead and had been for a long time; we wandered through Stockholm like a funeral cortège, my friends and I.

He said: "I pick girls up on the street as an experiment, a scientific approach to charting what goes on here. From work I head across Herkulesgatan, it's no big detour. You girls are always there, in different variations and constellations. As reliable as Jesus, simple and straightforward."

It is true. We come from nowhere, on our way to nowhere in particular. And money is something everyone understands. There is honour in it; it is untainted. And if one of us suddenly disappears, someone else will come. It is a space in perpetual motion, its door always open to all, where anything goes and where we always are. We expect nothing, we have nothing, we are simply there; and people can do with us what they will. We appeared like shadows in the street-light rain. A kind of forgiveness or comfort flowed from the holes in our bodies and I sometimes thought they came to us to weep. And afterwards we vanished back into the night from which we came. As if we surfaced the moment they noticed us. When they have discharged their effluent into us they want us to vanish, to remove our murky crevices, our averted eyes, and so we do, we absent ourselves, are gone. It is like going to confession, but without God.

"Look, I'm in heaven now," shouts Eskil, his mouth filled with river water. It is a heaven that has come loose from its mooring and rolled in underneath the black earth. When I look up there is no heaven and no Raksha, just an empty chasm where her eyes used to be, a yawning gorge that must be the entrance to the gates of hell.

It is always night-time in childhood. Eskil is standing by my bed again, his hair like a little halo of light round his head.

"Don't be cross, Inni, but I think I've wet the bed."

"It doesn't matter. As long as you're coming back."

But when I reach out for him he disappears and all that is left is the music and the crystalline light from the room next door. Where Raksha and Ivan are dancing their eternal waltz.

They tell me Eskil is in heaven now. But when I try to go to sleep at night, in the little interlude between wakefulness and dream, I hear his faint voice calling for me once again.

"I don't want to be on my own, Inni."

"You don't have to be on your own. You can stay here with me."

"But that's not possible."

"Of course it's possible. I can hold on to you like a balloon."

"There aren't any balloons here."

He is silent for a moment before saying any more. In the silence I can hear something coming that I won't like.

"I have to go back now, Inni."

"But I don't understand why."

"I don't either, but I have to follow the rules," he says and starts to cry.

"What rules? I don't want to follow any rules."

"I don't either, but we have to all the same."

After Eskil's death I was alone all the time. Alone with my kind, alone in my universe. But one day I discovered I did belong somewhere; I established contact with higher powers. I had fallen asleep by the river and when I woke and stood up, my shadow suddenly had wings. I stood absolutely still, staring at the pearl-grey angel wings quivering on the faded grass. Surrounding me was a strong smell of ether and marble and old feathers and the sound of furious fluttering overhead. When I turned, slowly as in a dream, a huge white bird of prey hung motionless in the air above me. The bird's wings in my shadow had made me look like an angel, that was all. It beat them hard to hover in the air before it flew off. But I never forgot it. I imagined I was in touch with something greater than myself and I too was an angel who could take my leave at any moment; I believed I was immortal. Now, I believe all the bird did was single me out for this hunter.

Massive cold clouds have formed over the frozen river and that year the first snow falls as early as September. It doesn't matter that Eskil is dead, as long as he comes home again in the end. He can be dead for a little while, I think, until we have changed, until we have mended our ways, become different people, less careless. After the funeral, I think, that is when he is going to come back. I look forward to the funeral, as if it were a party. But the funeral comes and goes without Eskil, and I realise that death wants something of us that we are not aware of, and I have to understand what it is. I am death's collateral.

"What's he wearing where he is now?" I ask Raksha.

"Nothing. We put his blanket in the coffin. That's enough. He has everything he needs now." Even though they are open, Raksha's eyes are closed, they no longer see anything. I would have liked that blanket back, as it does actually belong to me, but everyone has forgotten and I wouldn't want to be seen as a grave robber. It is bad enough that I want to dig him up and bring him home. I am worried he is frightened where he is now, in that unreachable heaven beneath us, that he is scared of the angels and the dark and the other dead people; I can picture old men and drunks and suicides roaming around down there. I imagine digging up his little coffin, taking him home and washing the earth out of his eyes.

The small black-clad troupe struggles against the wind with a coffin shining white in all the grey. Around us the world is cold, a dreadful '70s winter that kills everything. Eskil is under the ground by the church, and that is his place now, Ivan says. We are large ants carrying away our dead without understanding why we do it, just bearing them to a hole in the ground the gravedigger has opened. Everyone weeps apart from me, but something inside me has frozen. It isn't just the tears, it is something else. A disillusionment so deep, so penetrating, the freezing point of blood, the ultimate Antarctica of love.

Eskil doesn't exist anywhere in this world now. But he still comes to me in my dreams. I want to go to bed so that I can meet him and I start sleeping for several hours every day after school, but months pass before he shows himself again. At first I hear his voice but can't see him.

"I'm here Inni . . ."

"Look, Inni . . ."

"Don't be sad . . ."

"Here I am . . ."

I stand on the riverbank with the sun in my eyes. His little shadow appears further down on the shore. He has a bucket in his hand filled to the brim with water and when he runs it bounces and the water splashes out. He races towards me as usual, his arms outstretched, like a miniature aeroplane.

"Shall I show you how much I love you, Inni?"

I try to answer but my voice has died, gone, and just as I move to catch him in my arms and lift him up, he dissolves, like a soap bubble in my hand; and river water and ashes run through my fingers.

*

I would really like to speak to Eskil about what is happening now. About Raksha's silence, about the fact that she has stopped talking to me. As though I don't exist. Maybe she never did talk to me, but at least I had him then. I didn't know how much I needed that little kid. I am always waiting for him to get in touch. Can you make calls from the kingdom of the dead? Can you phone from heaven? If that is where he is. Not that he was in the habit of ringing me before; Eskil obviously didn't make a single phone call in his life, he was too young and he had no-one to ring, we were his whole world. That is the awful thing about families, they are your entire world, there is nothing beyond it. But I can imagine that the means for talking to the dead would be by telephone, and I think we should have made an arrangement, Eskil and I, for finding one another if anything happened. Like the game he loved where he hid and I found him. The one where I walked around searching and pretending I didn't see him, though he was very bad at hiding, always visible in his red dungarees, as conspicuous as a streak of blood in the snow. Sometimes I think the game is still going on, he has just got better at concealing himself. I keep expecting him to pop out from behind a tree by the river.

With time I forget how little he was when he was here, how difficult it would have been to make him understand instructions about life after death and that he would have had to commit everything we said to memory. Did we talk about death before he went? We spoke about the deaths of birds and rabbits and badgers and squirrels, but never about one of us dying.

*

The slope below the grave is bare, just the wind blowing through some trees and further down a man by himself waiting to place the headstone. A seabird flying overhead looks as though it is chasing sunbeams. When the gravedigger is ready he makes the sign of the cross and lowers the little coffin. And the earth swallows up its prey, because the soil is meagre and dry, in constant hunger. Eskil belongs to the church and the gravedigger now.

There are moments when I understand that he is ashes and dust, but I still keep asking, "Where is he now?" and Raksha withdraws from me even more. Soon she is a creature on another planet. And when she answers her voice sounds as though it is coming from a different world.

"He's in the ground."

"In the churchyard, among the graves? What about heaven?"

"Yes, heaven . . . Heaven . . ."

The road to heaven goes through the earth, she has already told me that many times before. That is why I am drawn there, as though by an immense magnetic force.

We stepped out of the car in a single movement. All thoughts of running had faded from my mind; any thoughts I still had were dragging so slowly, as if through water or mud, like waste matter passing through bowels. The trees bent in dark shadows over the lake and the reflection of the reeds made it look like they were growing in both directions, up into the sky and down into the water.

Surrounding the lake was a narrow, dismal shore of coarse-grained sand and black stones, there were streaks of gold in the motionless water and birds in the distance, birds that suddenly rose into the sky and were gone. Churned-up foam rippled at the water's edge; no other person had ever set foot here, on the last shore, or those who had could all be dead now and I would soon be one of them. He took out the knife. "It's time," he said in the same gentle voice they used in the office when they were forcing me to give up my child, when they finally demanded the keys to our apartment on Sockenplan. His jaw was so tight I could see the skull under his face, the skeletal shape, the crude outline of a human being, and I recall how Shane and I had laughed when we saw Valle for the first time, the little frame with its grey edges doing somersaults inside the screen on the maternity ward. "There, now," he murmured as he fumbled with his trousers, before he pushed his way into the empty hole between my legs. There was no pain, nothing mattered any more, this was the end; and I thought, the end comes as a release, the only mercy possible.

I looked up into the sky, so close, lowered like a face above me, like a stream of water suddenly flowing round me, and all I wished for was that I wouldn't wish for anything else. I had wished for the end and now it was here. And yet within me came the pleading, like a bullet from a gun. *Help me, God, whoever you are.* But it was no good. Darkness descended on the world as if someone had thrown a blanket over it.

"Help me, somebody . . ."

Earth spilled out when I opened my mouth, black mud poured out of me, silt and sludge and slime, but no-one could hear me; when I finally called out it was far too late.

"Go on, shout," he said, pulling my head back, and I could hear my screams, echoing across the lake water. Was it really me shouting? Yes, it was, for we were the only ones there, and although he hadn't yet chopped up my body, everything inside me – my voice and my thoughts – was already in pieces. This was what he had been waiting for, for me to beg for my life. A sign. My shouts died away, my head fell to the side and he shook my body as though he had changed his mind and needed to jolt me back to life; but I was no longer there. He bit me, scratched me with his nails, licked me like an old dog, as if he wanted me back.

Where is the sound of the twigs breaking when they strike my face? I can no longer hear it, the sounds are missing, only the taste of blood and metal and polluted rain in my mouth, and I feel nothing now, nothing hurts. *Do you hear, Raksha?*

I feel nothing now. Everything that was once important has ebbed away, like the tide, like the silvery magnetism of the old moon as it pulls everything towards it. Nothing can touch me now. Heroin takes it all; but when all the darkness is taken, so is all the light.

Just when you think the end has arrived, there is a pause, something in him or in time, a sudden inertia in all his movements. He looks up at the crown of the tree to which he has tied me, he looks over the forest, to the light flowing down from heaven onto the world, as if he is searching for something.

"What are you waiting for?" I want to ask, but there are no words left, all my words are pleas and I don't want to beg, not him, not anyone, I would rather perish than beg for anything. There are no clouds, only the smoky vault descending gently to earth. The last thing I want now is a chink to escape; I want it to be too late, for it to be over at last, for there finally to be something greater than my will. There is: he is holding his hands around my throat again now, and I see the sky above slide across as if on a platter, the vast expanse of the silver sky where all the colours run together like the ink in a water-stained drawing. Why is the sky never blue, why are there never blue skies, why are they only grey-tinged green and violet and yellow?

I see myself lying beneath the trees, collapsed in the mud. He is crouching, staring at me. He touches the bruise on my throat; it looks like a butterfly perching there. My jumper is ripped, my eyes still alive for a few seconds more before they become fixed. In an instant my body transforms into a photograph that has been tossed out onto the landscape, a stone or a leaf. He turns me over and uncovers my shoulders to reveal the marks of wings that have been torn off. It wasn't him; it was someone else who did it, a long time ago. And now, again, he takes out his knife and it shines like a mirror in his hand.

He drops my head into the old slurry pit – but I already told you that, didn't I? That there were such things in those days – because my neck bears the marks of his hands and nails. Then he positions the suitcases containing what used to be me along the motorway, so he can drive past every day and think of me and of what happened in the forest.

Ivan lay watching fleeting beads of light drip through the lowered blinds in Raksha's bedroom and Raksha lay beside him, watching him. When she closed her eyes she saw the birds of prey above the woods in Hägersten settle on the suitcase and try to retrieve the blood-soaked clods that lay inside.

"Why didn't he take her heart, Raksha?"

Ivan's head was in shadow. She took his cold hand and placed it against her cheek.

"I don't know. He didn't want it."

"But if her heart is still there, couldn't they wake her up again?" he whispered, and she thought he didn't mean what he was saying, but he said it all the same. And now he wept for the first time.

If I had still had my voice I could have told them that I hadn't had a heart for some time; I had a clenched, blood-soaked muscle under my ribs, but I didn't feel anything anymore. That was what I had striven for, for heartlessness.

"She's no Snow White," Raksha said softly, "and really we lost her a long time ago."

Raksha used to read *Snow White* to me. She read other things as well, but that was the story we liked best. When Snow White's mother tells the huntsman to take Snow White out into the forest and kill her and bring back her heart as proof, a shiver of ice ran through me and I stared up at Raksha to see how she looked, to see if she was transmuting into someone else, but it was the same large, intent face suspended above me like my personal moon. And when Snow White promised the huntsman she would go into the forest and never return if he would only spare her life, her eyes glistened.

"I don't think it's her," Ivan said.

"Then you'll just have to trust me."

"How can I do that?"

Raksha sat up and placed her arms around his back.

"Do you remember that mark on her shin? The one that looked like a little heart?"

It was something they had said to one another a long time ago: one of the gods hadn't been able to resist drawing a tiny heart on me before sending me down to Raksha and Ivan. A little stamp of soft pink. Raksha continued.

"I've seen the mark on a photograph. And they had her fingerprints. I didn't want to say before. Or I didn't understand that we really were searching for her, you and I. And she had a small rose tattooed on her back. She had it done last year when she was pregnant. I've seen that as well. We have to stop searching, Ivan. Do you understand?"

Ivan turned away from her.

When he came out into the kitchen it was so late, darkness had already started to fall. Usually he would get up first, he always woke early and padded around the apartment, waiting for her to rise. It had only been a few weeks, but they already had their ways, and on this day she was the one waiting for him. He sat hunched by the window and drank his coffee without looking at her.

"I'm going out by myself today," he said, standing up.

"But I want to come with you."

"You can't. I have to go by myself."

"I can't be alone. I think I'll die if you leave me now."

She took his hand in hers and I knew she had always loved his big hands. They contained all the sensitivity he refused to acknowledge. He left his hand in hers, like a stone, he didn't move it, didn't answer. She went down on her knees and begged him to stay with her, but he walked away. Still without looking at her. And he didn't come back that evening. But he left his things in the bedroom. A suitcase and some plastic bags and a china dog he had bought in a flea market.

Ivan roamed around Haga Palace in the moonlight. In the background he could hear the gentle hum of the motorway. A narrow strip of shore below the palace, which was in darkness now, and further along grass and trees and occasional street lamps and the light streaming from the little temple. He thought he was walking around searching for the child that society had thrown away. Those people up there took better care of their dogs than they had of his child. In a way it made me happy that Ivan was sad because I was dead, but I wished he would leave it alone now, I wanted him to take care of Raksha. But all I could do was follow at a distance as he ran and stumbled on the muddy wet grass. I saw him stand up again and run on, from one end of the palace to the other, towards the motorway.

One night he walked up to Herkulesgatan. Light shone from the banks' windows, and the open mouths of the multi-storey carparks ejected the balmy air that used to keep us warm when it was cold. And that is how it is: at first we are invisible and then we are everywhere, huddled in our padded jackets and furs, frozen, waiting. Blank, eyeless buildings, the scent of eau-de-Cologne and patchouli, and after a while the men who step out like shadows from the architecture. Nanna stood alone on the pavement with a tape recorder beside her and a globe under her arm, wearing a hat I had never seen before.

The globe was bright blue and the flex trailed behind her when they walked away. They walked away together.

In the soft glow from a night lamp in a hotel room by Tegnér-lunden she takes something, as soon as they have come through the door, with her pants pulled down over both of her hips and one of her buttocks. Ivan looks away when she pushes the needle through her skin, and she waits for it to arrive in her heart. When she has finished, she collapses onto the floor, lying like a bundle of rags under the window, not unconscious but unreachable, and he lifts her onto the bed. For several moments he gazes at her lying on the bedspread; she must be asleep or perhaps just keeping her eyes shut, but they move like small living creatures under her eyelids. She has a large scratch on her neck, a blood-red weal, as if made by a claw. Gently he rolls down her tight jeans. I know that lying there she is floating in another world, a better world.

When there is nothing left on her lower body apart from a pair of faded knickers, he turns on the bedside lamp, removes the shade and passes the naked bulb back and forth over her legs. I realise he is trying to find that little heart that once was on my leg. He turns on the ceiling light, but still finds nothing; he runs his hands up and down her legs. When he turns her over she smiles and mumbles something. I think she is like an angel lying there, an angel just fallen from heaven.

Her breathing was so light, so imperceptible, and night crept into the room and filled it. Nanna looked so very young when I saw her with him, intensely vulnerable and innocent. When it was fully dark and only shafts of yellow light filtered in from the street and the buildings opposite, he stood up and took off all his clothes and left them lying by the bed. In the half-dark it looked as though someone must have squatted there and left a little pile of turds. He lay down behind Nanna and fell asleep.

He never came back to Raksha. Having waited for weeks, she went to the station and took a seat on a high-speed train south and then walked all the way to the apartment block by the river where, in another century, she had once lived. From inside the apartment she could hear the sound of the television, but he didn't open the door. In a broken voice she shouted through the letterbox, but there was no reply. She sank to the cold floor and sat motionless, but for the slight movement of her eyelids in the darkness. Sometimes the light went on in the entrance hall and she blinked at the fluorescent lamp for a few moments before it went dark again. She sat in the corridor, freezing in her thin coat, her teeth chattering, like a little animal. I believed it was my fault she was sitting there, but I couldn't help her. If only I could have told her Ivan was sitting on the other side of the door, listening to her breaths.

After two days she took the train back. The journey was quiet, she was alone in the carriage for most of the way, sitting by the window in the bright sunlight and seeing the trees thin out until they disappeared completely and were replaced by bare, drab landscape. She imagined she was bound for the under-world, that the conductor who periodically swayed through the carriage was her escort. He smiled at her every time he passed, as though he had personal charge of her journey. Perhaps she had never properly left that first time many years before. She had walked away from Ivan then, with me at her side, in the belief that she was saving us from something, at least that is the way I see it, that she left so that I would escape their war, but Raksha's life thereafter had just become a period of waiting for him to come after her, of waiting to experience again the shining light she had once experienced with him. Now she was really leaving, without the hope that he would come running. She believed she was on her way home at last, that nothing was waiting for her, that what had begun one night at a fairground in Ängelholm twenty-five years earlier was finally over.

Only children believe we can have everything we wish for, but I sometimes think there is no such thing as children, the idea of the child is simply an illusion. So-called children are merely smaller in size and more easily deceived, they live with adults under duress, like any cuddly toy or pet. You hold out a dog-eared photograph of a gleaming baby, so people will think you are virtuous. As I did, thinking I was the Virgin Mary in the beginning when I was out pushing Valle in his pram, when he was newborn. But a human is neither good nor evil; she is like a wasp, part of the ecosystem.

There was a curse on our family. With the huge waterfalls and the polluted water came the darkness, and it kept on flowing through the generations. When I was a child I believed I would be able to lift that curse, but then I went along with it instead. It was so easy, there was a golden line to follow, as plain as the river lying heavy on the landscape.

It is very easy to kill someone, so much easier than you might imagine. I think that was what he said. It was the only thing that surprised me, his sentimentality, his difficulty in letting me go, his unwillingness to leave me there by the lake. Why did I go with him? I went with him because I knew he wanted to kill me. I recognised him the minute he appeared in the street; there was something about his eyes, he looked like anybody else, even attractive, but his eyes were like a reptile's or a dragon's, glinting cold. Everyone on the street knew who he was, and everyone was afraid of him, avoided him and his car; but not I.

I always liked the idea of dying by my own hand, of taking control of my own life, the only way of rebelling against the world. But the truth is I was too weak to put the knife to my throat myself. And I always knew I would die young. This is eternity without me.

LONGING

Lake Vättern lies like a gash in the landscape, a gigantic water-filled groin that opens up when you come down the E4 motorway from the north. It is one of Europe's largest lakes and little Solveig walks along the shore every morning with her satchel. I have seen her going back and forth between the house in the forest and the school beside the deep lake. She is constantly sidetracked and is always late, because she keeps finding things. She has coins and stones and other treasures hidden in every drainpipe. She knows nothing other than life here, in this little town with a church on every corner, where the houses rise steeply up the mountain sides; round her neck she wears a silver cross that she touches when she is anxious. She prays to God every night, not because she believes in God, but because that is what you do here. She prays for puppies and kittens and white parrots. Her world is filled with small animals, just like Valle's, cats and deer and foals and little birds, an entire Disney World.

The shimmering blue mountains all around mean that it is always cold; the town lies trapped in shadow and the lake is never warm, even in summer, for it is so deep, over a hundred metres at its deepest. Solveig knows that she was born of wolves and that a human family has taken mercy upon her. She knows I am dead, but not how, and she knows that Shane has gone, but not why. And this is what hell is, watching your children live on without you. You think you will escape the sentence by dying, by being murdered and dismembered and dumped in white suitcases and eaten by flies, but it isn't enough. The punishment is having to watch, without the ability to get involved. But the truth is, life is better for them now that I am no longer part of it.

Valle has already moved numerous times and I think he struggles, though he never says anything; he would never complain or make a fuss, but several times I have seen him crying when he is on his own. He mostly keeps to himself and no-one seems particularly attached to him, neither children nor adults. Perhaps it is because he forgets to wipe his nose and round his mouth, and he always has a streak of milk and snot on his upper lip. Maybe it is because he eats faster than the others and with his mouth open, maybe it is because he has grown rather fat. Only a mother could love him. He sleeps on a rug outside his foster parents' bedroom, because he is still too frightened to sleep alone. Like a little dog. We are the ones who made him scared of the night.

It was a dog that discovered me, but sooner or later I would have been found by a person, given that the suitcases were so close to a human thoroughfare. It was as if he wanted everyone to see me, to see what he had done. In the late autumn of the first year he hung my bra on a sapling close to the place where one of the suitcases lay, but the snow came early and when it melted my bra was gone. He kept some of my things and buried them in a wood close to the house where he lived at the time. A small mirror, my earring and a stocking, which swiftly decomposed, like a flower. I think he wanted to sink back into the mire where his soul belonged, he wanted to come forward, to be punished, but his courage failed him.

He preserved his memories as I preserve mine. For him I was the writing on the landscape, a secret message for an undisclosed recipient. I still don't know what the message was. We know nothing of what is in a person's heart, we can only guess. It would have been better if I had disappeared without trace, if no-one had needed to see my dead body; it wasn't even a body anymore, it was offal, carrion, shapeless lumps as far from their origins as the body parts glistening in the refrigerated cabinet at the cash-and-carry.

The crowns of the trees above are moving; it looks as though they have come unmoored and are drifting on the white surface of the sky, as if the sky itself were an immense lake in which the treetops are being drawn irresistibly to its murky depths, leaving the roots floating on the top like massive black hands reaching for heaven. I think it must be the birch trees tinkling like a thousand tiny bells and making a speckled dance of light that stipples his freckled hands. And now the numbness comes, spreading through my body in swirls of gurgling silver, it comes when there is no more chance of escape and I feel as though snowflakes are falling inside me. A feeling so raw, so pure, so cold, transcending anything I have ever known.

A tremor passes across the lake, an invisible wind ruffing and scuffing the mirrorlike surface. When I try to say something, blood spills from my mouth. It doesn't matter, in any case it is too late to say anything now. This is death's vantage point, the hunter's angle. My body lies on the grass, a leather glove turned inside out. The eyes of the body on the grass are half-closed but there is still a glimmer of light beneath the eyelids. Why does that not go out, if it is all over anyway? And where is the blood coming from? Bright red foam at my mouth and he hasn't used the knife yet. And now the world is finally slipping away, like a ship, or a sandcastle swallowed up by the tide. Just as Eskil slipped from my hands so long ago. Brown water flooding the world, running into my eyes, death filling my veins and everything else, the layers of tissue in the orbs of my eyes, the ragged membranes in my lifeless womb, a mounting black slime slowly smothering my vision. Retina and sky merge into one, black ink overflows from the glass that is the world. His face is still hovering above me like a mirage, an image that jumps and shudders and shakes, as if someone has cut into your gaze with a knife, or sliced into the very perspective. I will pray to anyone at all now, I want an angel to come and devour me, I want darkness to surround me, for light and time to vanish from my eyes. I see everything slip away, the grass and the trees and the little slope down to the lake and the firmament above me with a scattering of clouds sliding slowly past in the opposite direction. Now his face is my entire universe, the only thing filling my eyes. The intense grey of the gaze, the prominent bridge of the aquiline nose, lips that are flat and half-open and saliva dripping onto my naked face, water coursing from the openings for his eyes and the dark hole of his mouth. I wish my last picture could be something other than this, a tree or a flower or Raksha's face from long ago, but it is too late for wishes now. And I hear Raksha's prayers running through me like old rosary beads. But I have never believed in God and God has never believed in me and I never wanted to be saved; nothing scared me like salvation. *So see me now, Raksha, as I walk into death, as I walk into the murderer's world, see how I walk in with open eyes. See me now, Raksha, as I soar into the heavens never to return.*

The ripples on the water have settled into a mirror surface of leaden gold, the setting sun behind the pine trees, the birds caught in a wing-beat. Every image is frozen, like my body, rigid, fixed, a photograph. Like the pictures of me that will appear later in the newspapers. The black-and-white one where I have permed hair and eyes as deep as graves; I look bloody awful, but Shane said it made me look like Bambi. We took that picture in a photo booth on Kungsholmen.

He must have picked up the knife, for then small droplets of blood flew through the air, some as tiny as pinheads, sombre spatter on sombre sand. Soon I was lying on the shore in seven pieces. Soon he had scooped out my womb and pulled out my intestines. The world was broken now, seven fragments of mirror lying on the grass, seven bits of heaven reflected, seven sections of the hunter's unknown face. That is why it is so hard to remember; because all experience comes piecemeal. It has always been this way. There is never a complete picture of the world, never a single picture. Something in my vision began to tremble and spin before the picture could appear and then there was no picture at all. Just slivers of reflected light and voices and wisps of heaven. But now I was rendered harmless, no more images would come to me, and nor would I try to say anything else. Tongue cut out, head tossed into the sludge, face streaked with mud and grit.

*

I think of Valle when he was newly born, how quiet he was. I was waiting for the cry but it didn't come. Why isn't he screaming, I asked the midwife. She shook her head and smiled, wrapped him in a blanket and laid him down with me. As if she didn't know the answer either. But he was alive, he was lying there with his round eyes looking up at me, he was breathing, he was moving his little hands, they were opening and closing. He didn't ever cry much afterwards either, just lay quietly in his crib under the window, looking up at the sky, as if he already knew he was alone in the world.

And now? Now he places what is left of me in two suitcases and puts them into the boot of the car. My blood is still on the earth like a shadow, but the earth here is mostly sand and ancient shells and it will soon sink in. He stares out across the water, calm and focussed, so much in the moment that the colours of the landscape assume uncommon depth, and everything strikes him with intensity, sharpness, like the reflection of something not of this world, the smell of water and earth and blood, the sound of the torpid lake water, the lapping of tiny waves. If anyone had asked him he would simply say he was performing a deed everyone else would have liked to do; make me dissolve, turn into earth and flesh and matter for the stars, put out the light in my eyes definitively. Someone has to do it, and he is the one with the courage. That is how he would explain it, if anyone asked. But no-one ever does.

After we die, the place we occupied in the world is filled by the living sooner than you would think. It doesn't take long, something to do with time and gravity and how your space immediately contracts, seeming to shrink, in the end eliminating the room we took up on earth. Even if the laws of physics had been on my side, it would have been impossible for me to return. If I suddenly showed up at Valle's and Solveig's, they wouldn't recognise me, although they think they miss me. What they miss is an old fairy tale that finished long ago. Valle remembers us, but his memories are mere snatches now. They nestle inside him like glassy wicked stones and he brings them out as seldom as he can. Perhaps so that they won't wear thin.

I try to find a bright memory inside him, but there are none. None in me, and none in him. I don't know if it is because shadows always gather in memories. Or maybe the occasional bright moments don't count in the great darkness of what is left of our lives. I couldn't look at photographs of him even when he was living with Shane and me. Not even on the good days, and there were such days as well. Many days were full of brightness, untainted, many days I would stay away from all the bad; and we had a good time, Valle and Shane and I. Even if it was sometimes boring in the way it is with a child when you stand pushing a swing in some godforsaken playground, though in your heart of hearts you are filled with tremulous, whirling joy at the beauty, light and miracle of your child's being. But in all the baby pictures in our photograph album, Valle looked so alone and helpless, as if trapped and defeated by the camera's empty flash and the very idea of being a baby. I can still see the little quiver of the dummy when he had sucked so hard and created a vacuum that finally relaxed.

Even in those days I would start weeping the moment I opened our album because I felt sorry for him sitting locked in the picture, sucking on his plastic dummy, and I couldn't reach him, couldn't comfort him. The photographs were time that had passed and had made the undone done. And so it still is. Where have those albums gone now? I have no idea what happened to all our things after my death. It doesn't matter, here you have no need of things, and maybe it is just as well they have gone. Valle and Solveig have created new pictures, they have new family trees.

The earth's surface is covered with the dead; we are a dark mixture of ash and gases and organic material that you tread on every day. Certainly not on purpose, but it is a fact, every day you tread on us and force us deeper and deeper into the earth. The living have always been afraid of the dead, but there is nothing to fear, our space on earth is soon filled by those who are left. Just look at Solveig on the sofa, lying on Ellen's knee with her eyes closed with the news on in the background. There are reports on the television of blood and earth and mortality and tonight there has also been an item about me. It isn't a problem, because Solveig isn't listening and anyway she doesn't know it concerns the person who was once her mother. I hope she never finds out. There is no place for me in the house by Lake Vättern; Solveig is consumed with the people around her, Ellen and Johan, whose love will come to be a shining light inside her. I often wonder who has taken my place on the street, who is looking after Nanna, and I wonder if anyone rings Raksha now that I never do.

I come to them in their dreams. I blow gently on Solveig's face as she sleeps, but perhaps I just drive more and more shadows into her when I try to fill her with light. I wish I could give her a heart that can endure both love and tragedy.

Sometimes when I am there she wakes up and calls for her mother, and, because I can't reply, soon the other mother is sitting by her bed.

"Were you calling?"

"I dreamed you'd gone."

"But I'm here. I'm always here."

As a mother you have to last at least twenty years, and that is a long time, but I think Ellen is the type who will manage it. She has an inner calm and as she says now in the dark of the night, she is always there for Solveig and the other children. Perhaps she does slightly prefer her own children, her birth children, but I hope Solveig also arouses a special tenderness, as she lies in bed, warm and soft, stretching out her arms to be picked up even though she is really too big. Her eyes are pale blue, her mouth as small as a woodland strawberry.

"What happened to . . . to my . . . mother?" she might suddenly ask on such a night, and each time the question makes her more uneasy, since after all her mother is sitting right beside her on the bed, Ellen's cloudless face floating above her like a lantern in the half-dark room.

"Was she very lonely?"

"Yes."

Every time Solveig wakes at night and asks for me, I think I will have to stay away in future. All I have to give her is anxiety and broken sleep. They have told her I was ill, but she seems dissatisfied with the answer, as if she knows instinctively it isn't true.

"Why couldn't they make her well again?"

"She was very poorly and in the end her heart gave out," Ellen says, stroking Solveig's soft cheek and glancing aside, the way you do when you tell a lie. And it is obvious she can't tell the truth. But I'm still sad. Your mother is a mound of flesh in the forest, Solveig, I whisper.

And I am grateful, I really am. I could never have given Solveig everything she has now. It is difficult to explain. It is not that it is clean, because it isn't, we made everything cleaner than this, Shane and I; we were constantly cleaning, like maniacs. But there is a tranquillity about these people. Trivial things, like Ellen taking the time to fill a spray bottle with half washing-up liquid and half water, to save on the washing-up liquid. That sort of thing shows attention to detail. She takes her time, she isn't on edge. She and Johan are in a place they want to be and they are not going anywhere else. She can't imagine another life. This is enough for them: to be woken early by the blare of an alarm clock and go to work in the care service and the library and come home again to cook a meal and clean the house and play with Solveig and the other children. Ellen and Johan find beauty and order in the world and have a natural place in it. In my head I had hundreds of plans for different lives and didn't know which of them to seize upon. And so I seized on none.

"And then I came to you," Solveig whispers in the small vestige of night still resting upon her room like a gossamer of blue. She is soon sleeping again. Peaceful and safe in the house by Lake Vättern. A light pours from the black water at night, as if a higher being lives deep in the lake. I don't hear what Ellen says in reply, for when she says it I have already left.

I am the one bringing troubled dreams to her, the silent wing-beats of the night. No, I have no wings. It is just a metaphor. But sometimes in the past it did feel that way, that there was something monstrous moving on my back, as if there were an alien presence within me that would force its way out between my shoulder blades at any moment.

Sometimes I used to think that Valle would be fine regardless, that someone touched by a love like Shane's and mine would never forget it; it was like an elixir or a shining aura that would always have an effect on him. Now I think the elixir we passed on to him was harmful. Our desperation and disquiet flows through him. Our longing for death.

I can still hear Shane's voice, though he left me a long time ago, but his voice remains inside me, like the soft purl of water. Or was it I who left him? You leave each other so many times before you finally go, in the end you don't remember who left whom. Perhaps it was love that left us both, it tired of us and moved along. I don't think we deserved it. Whatever love is. I think it is a place in the light where nothing can catch you.

Solveig often says it. "And then I came to you . . . And then I came to you . . . And then I came to you . . ." As if, by repeating it, she will understand where she comes from. Maybe she is only trying to erase what was there before, to create her own lineage, starting from when Ellen and Johan appear. Certainly, she was in my womb for months, but it could have been anyone's. She must have heard my voice and Shane's, but she would doubtless have heard many other voices. The women at the local authority office; a variety of people in the street talking bullshit right next to my enormous stomach. And those two hours at the hospital after the birth when she lay and looked up at me, only I remember those. For her that time is gone.

Valle is alone in the forest in Havsmon with his knives and in the half-light of dusk he appears lit up from within, like a little cherub. No-one has taken my place in his life; he is still waiting for someone to love him.

He is so like me, it frightens me sometimes. I can see the deep pit inside him, opening and closing. I daren't look in on him, I imagine I would destroy something. His existence is so fragile, the eczema makes him sore and he finds it difficult to sleep at night because he has such dark dreams. The nightmares come from Shane and me. I have seen inside those terrible dreams, seen him hunted by a pack of wolves that want to kill him. The wolves are us and we come out every night. If I had a gun I would shoot them.

At school he is on his own, no-one ever speaks to him. When he asks if he can join in, the others just shrug their shoulders and carry on as they were, and Valle doesn't know what to do. Other kids take a shrug like that as permission to participate, but not Valle. He tries to walk quietly away so that no-one will notice him. He hides his loneliness from his new parents; he knows that no-one likes a boy without friends. Sometimes he stays out in the afternoons and says he has been at a friend's house. Then he will go into the forest, sit on the big stone by the lake and whittle sticks into weapons. I don't want him to carry a knife, but it makes him feel safe to have it in his rucksack, shining, wrapped in newspaper. At dusk he returns to the house in Havsmon and has the same feeling he has at school, of not being truly present for the others there. They are never unkind to him, never a bad word, but they see him come and go as though he doesn't really exist in their world. Every day newly pressed clothes are hanging by the side of his bed. They often ask him if he needs anything, but he doesn't understand the question and would never think of anything he needed of his own volition. If it weren't for the dogs he would run away. It is the only time he is happy, when he is with the dogs in the forest, when they run towards him through the trees so fast that all four paws leave the ground. Does he remember the dogs we used to play with on Floragatan? Does he remember that he once lived with wolves?

He has already moved many times. He has only lived with these new people for a year. The house in Havsmon isn't very far from Solveig's, just a few miles north. Neither knows of the other's existence; I don't think anyone told them they have a brother or sister. Perhaps it is just as well, as they wouldn't be able to find each other anyway.

I would say to Valle and Solveig that if they don't see any point to all of this, to all the hurt that always hurts, to the impossibility of the three of us ever being together, it is because there isn't any point. I believe that in the end what matters is accepting your place in creation. You have to learn to love your fate, or at least accede to it, regardless of its price, regardless of its hell.

There was only the two of us now. I imagined my grave would be the lake, that he would drag my body into the water and let it sink. I pictured Eskil sitting on the lake bed waiting for me, so I felt no fear. The effort to live as the creature someone had once made me, God or Raksha or Ivan or whoever it was, the creature I had never managed to be, was over now.

Drowning is said to be a gentle death, almost erotic. But the body doesn't want to die, it can't give up, its every fibre is focussed on survival. It is a human pretence, to say that death is like falling asleep. It isn't like that even for those who die in hospital; they suffocate slowly, as if smothered by giant hands.

But drowning was not to be my fate, for now he was strangling me by the water's edge. That was what he had been waiting for. Finally he was equal to the gods. I too had been waiting, waiting for someone with the courage to kill me.

I assume it was something he wished to prove to the world. His strength, and the inner resemblance to a god that only he knew of. When we drove through the forest I had been frightened, but when we reached the shore the fear had vanished. I stepped out of the car as if I had already arrived in the kingdom of the dead. Weightless, speechless, cold. I lay down on the shore on a blanket that he fetched from the car and he wasn't instantly transformed before my eyes. His gaze didn't darken with hatred the way it sometimes could with some of the men on the street, when my naked body and my naked face suddenly filled them with rage. This one was still as a lizard before he throttled me, his touch on my body cautious, bloodless, slightly awkward. Then he lay on top of me and tightened his hands around my neck. I didn't scream, because I couldn't, my vocal chords were ragged and I was bleeding all over my lungs.

Valle ran away and when he was found in Stockholm the people in Havsmon didn't want him back.

"We don't think it's a good idea," they said, wringing their hands.

"Children in this situation often run away," said the woman in the social services office who was responsible for him now. "It's a way of testing you. To see if you really want him."

Valle was sitting in the next room, waiting, but they didn't know that. He didn't hear what they said, but through the wall he felt the frostiness grow, felt the chill radiating from the room. The couple looked down at the table, their hands entwined.

"No, we don't believe he wants to be in Havsmon. And the truth is we can't cope with him anymore."

From the room next door Valle saw the pair from Havsmon being led along the corridor, their eyes cast down to the floor. He thought about the dogs and wished he could have taken them with him to wherever he was going next. He thought more of the dogs than they did. They showed the same cool friendliness to the animals as they did to him. If only he could have gone back and stolen those dogs.

Someone came into the room and told him he was going to be driven to a temporary family in Vallentuna where he would stay until a new home was found. Valle walked out to the taxi and immediately fell asleep on the back seat. When he woke two strangers were staring in through the window. All he hoped for was dogs, that these people would have dogs too. But the new people had no dogs and the silence spread like a vapour through the rooms. He didn't know what to do with himself in the house and he felt as though he was being watched as he sat on the edge of the chair, waiting. They asked what he intended to do with his life. He had no idea, he was eleven, he didn't even know what he was going to do with the next hour. Did he ever think about us, about Shane and me? We were no more than a flickering candle inside him that he could never really grasp, a warmth seeping up. There was so much time that only I could remember, existing in him as mere slivers of light. I hope he had my love in his soul, the love from the first years of his life; I wish it could stay inside him like a protective serum. But I often think it must be the reverse, that we have poured poison into him and this is what prevents him accepting the loving care of these people. That must be it, but the thought is so painful it flies away before it can take hold.

I used to hate the people who had assumed responsibility for Valle and Solveig, I despised their smugly virtuous lives, the fact they could already have so much, they had surplus to give to an unknown child. Now I hate only myself. I see Valle sitting in his clean, sunshine-yellow room in Vallentuna, not touching the things they have given him, not daring to move anything from its original place. He makes his own bed every morning without anyone asking him to and the only things in the room he picks up are the dog posters that belong to him and he can look at them for hours. The people have suggested he could put them up on the wall, said it might be nice to have them framed, but he doesn't want to. He wants to be able to get hold of them quickly if anything were to happen, if he suddenly had to leave again. There are children in the house, but they are old, teenagers, always on their way out somewhere. They call him their little kid brother, knock on his door and come in to look at the dog pictures, but after a while it goes quiet, they walk off and Valle is left alone in the room he dare not touch. Sometimes the older ones have presents, small things, cheap, but nonetheless: a packet of chewing gum, a bouncy ball, a Disney comic. In the mornings Valle is so quiet that in the room around him a circle forms and becomes impossible to penetrate. Every time he attempts to say something his face fills with blood and every time it gets harder. They let him be and in the end they forget he is there. All the time he has that comic-book sense of there being five mistakes in the room to spot: his head, both his arms and his legs hanging point-lessly over the chair with feet that don't even reach the floor. No-one says it out loud, but it is as clear to him as if they had shouted in his ear.

When he ran away from Havsmon he regretted it instantly, but he couldn't go back because he was ashamed. He didn't ever want to leave the dogs. He travelled by train to Stockholm and walked around for days before they found him. Something draws him back to the city and I suspect it might be Shane and me. If only I could make him understand there is nothing here, that under its elegant surface the city is raw and dangerous. I hope he doesn't run away this time, but I recognise the instinct to flee, the desire to escape from the world the moment it comes close. Inside, he is already on the run. When he lies in bed in the afternoons he is in another world, a world I hope doesn't claim him completely. It is like a drug and it makes me frightened. So I look away.

One day, when I had just begun to show, we went to the social services office, Shane and I. It was quite a while before it was outwardly noticeable though, because I was so thin. I think Solveig was trying to hide away from us in there, and I can understand why, we had nothing to offer her on the other side. We told them the truth, that everything was falling apart and they would have to take her as well. In fact, Shane and I didn't see eye to eye; he thought I was awful, I was giving up too easily. Maybe I was, but he didn't know what it felt like with the needle against my vein, aware of the baby fluttering inside and not knowing if it was withdrawal or my anxiety that was waking her out of her dormancy. He didn't know what the danger felt like sweeping through my blood into hers, surging straight from paradise into me and making her quiet. Into us, for it was the same sick blood that flowed between us; we were still as one.

I had taken drugs when I was pregnant with Valle too. But that time I didn't know what was in store, I didn't know that I was carrying inside me a real child with bright eyes and a ticking heart and breath of untouchable delicacy. Valle had been the child who was going to change everything; and he had changed nothing.

After we had signed the papers Shane stayed away more and more, and when he was there he didn't look at me, he looked at something further away in the room. I wasn't taking anything now. I drank from time to time, vodka or red wine, and I took a few pills, but none of the things I craved. I lay in bed for days on end, watching the sky skim along outside and feeling the baby move inside me, first like a spider and later like a little fish or seal. An elbow, a knee, the weight of the head between my legs, and we spoke to each other wordlessly as I lay on my side with my hand pressed to my stomach, as if goading her until she kicked back. Solveig was born that same year on New Year's Eve.

It was one of the first warm summer nights, when the heat lingered long after the sun had gone down, hanging like a haze on the asphalt far into the night. When I had seen him circling us for a while, I walked over, bent down and met his eye on the other side of the car window, and when he had lowered it, in an infinitely slow electric motion, I asked him to take me somewhere.

"Where do you want to go?" he asked.

"Away from here," I said.

And when he leaned across and opened the door I entered his kingdom. It was like stepping into a different world. Inside the car it was still and oppressive, sun-hot seats, stifling air, classical music coming softly out of the radio. He said nothing, he didn't look at me, and I don't think I even said my name, perhaps he already knew what I was called. He put his foot gently on the accelerator and we moved smoothly away past the bank headquarters and the multi-storey car parks. And I saw it all for one last time: the girls standing around in their short fur jackets and their tights, smoking their way through the night. Above every girl hung a little cloud of smoke like an umbrella. I imagined it was Nanna leaning against the entrance door to the bank, an open book in her hand, but when we drove past I could see it wasn't her. And I thought how much I loved those girls, loved them for their simplicity and sensitivity, for being quite unafraid, and only here with them had I felt loved. It was the last thought I had, before we joined the motorway and drove on into the wide night.

I tried to say something when he entered me, but when I opened my mouth earth spilled out.

My soul had been loosened from its moorings many times and I had been in that floating place, looking down on myself, but this time I wasn't coming back. I knew that he would kill me, knew that I was going to die. A storm passed through his body, something shaking him, perhaps just the rush of orgasm. Saliva dribbled from his mouth onto my face. And the pictures came faster now, flickering shreds, black cracked mirrors, huge arrows fired into me from a giant bow far away. Who aims pictures at us from far-flung worlds? Pictures that will become our lives. Like the picture of me as an insect, ravaged by unseen wounds and injuries, a subhuman filled to the brim with filthy lake water threatening to spill out at any moment and drown everything around me. Is it Ivan's picture? Or Raksha's? Or is it the blessings and curses of the gods? You run into the arms of death, you seek a huntsman and a slaughterman. There is no way to withstand what lies ahead. And then he picked up the knife again, and I thought that was a good thing, for no-one would recognise me now, no-one would be able to identify me as anything other than earth, blood, waste. I had come into the wrong world, where I was never meant to be. I wanted it to be as if I were never there.

The sound of my heart beating across the landscape is deafening, and then it stops. I see the world around me disappear. It doesn't hurt. It doesn't matter anymore.

The only thing he kept at his own house was an earring. Doubtless he still has it, though probably stored away in a safe place. Perhaps he buried it in a plant pot so it would be close at all times; it was right by him on the occasions he was questioned by a police officer over my death. Yes, there was just the one earring, I only ever had one, in my right ear, a butterfly earring Shane gave to me. There was nothing symbolic about it. I don't even like butterflies. They are insects in disguise. He wanted to keep something, as a denial of total separation. I have realised, now that I have had the time to study them, that this is why murderers often slip up. They get caught because they find it difficult to say goodbye, they linger at the scene, leave clues on the body and take all kinds of trivial things. A lock of hair, a skull, or, in my case, an earring and the key to a locker at T-Centralen station, where I kept all my worldly goods. They were few in number, but they were mine. He never used the key; he threw it into Strömmen Bay and before long they opened the locker and disposed of my things. My suede jacket and bicycle key, my big tape recorder and the little plastic wristband they give you in hospital so that you don't lose track of your baby.

I remember the smell of that night. The stench of blood. The smell of genesis, the primeval odour of birth. Lake water. The same as the smell in the delivery room, around newborn infants. Seaweed and algae. Blood and excrement. Solveig exuded an intoxicating fragrance, as though someone had just lifted her out of a lake; but two hours later she was gone. That final night in the world, I remember the reek of lake and old vomit assailing me, the evening light hurtling down between the trees and the faint whir of the electricity cables above us. And the luscious scent of June, when the air is sated with moisture and sweetness and newly formed blossom.

June is the month of madness, when the sky is never dark; when sexuality, the beast within, awakens; when the flowers and caterpillars burst out of their cocoons and swaddling-clothes, brimming with chlorophyll and lust for life; and when the hunger stirs in creatures such as him to rape and strangle someone. But never will you find the person you are all searching for, never will you discover who he was. Someone picked me up in the twilight on Herkulesgatan one night in June; someone was with me in those last hours by the edge of the lake in the forest. Man and beast became one that night by the lake, I believe.

People say the dead know everything, and only the dead know the truth, or at least we think we do, and that makes us quite irritating. It gives us a superior attitude, unconstrained by fear of losing something, for we have lost everything already, even ourselves. Living a lie is over, the words speak for themselves. And maybe we do know a little more, since we have so much time to take a look around, when every moment stretches to a thousand years in the special time prevailing here. We see everything we didn't see before; whenever we return we hear new things, we see the fall of light a little more clearly and it has always shifted slightly since the last time we looked. Later when we are given passage, we revert to what came before, to the great anonymity, to the chain of life and rebirth that the body is part of, and we become flowers, trees, worms, butterflies. At best. Very likely most of us become ash and stardust. But you have to be patient, you must wait for permission to pass. The last time someone speaks our name on earth, we get our leave to travel. There is no need to stay any longer, we are authorised to sink back into what came before. The silence, of eternity. That is what we hope for. Yet no-one who loves me mentions me anymore. It is others who prattle on, people who write in the newspapers, folk who know all about everything. But I can't help hoping that someone will utter my name, that Valle will suddenly say "Mamma" and mean me.

*

It is the same with the murder series constantly on television, people in them spouting off all the time. Sometimes they catch my eye when I go past. Everything on television is about murder now. I don't know why, but people seem to love it. It is no different on there: the police officers and criminologists each acting as some kind of hero, sitting in immaculate rooms, with sleek hairdos, discussing the killer. And meanwhile my world is conjured up, and ever so subtly beside their glossy world a dangerous underworld emerges. Full of junkies, whores, crooks and other desperados. It tends to be the extras who play those parts. But really the only person of interest to them is the murderer, and of course the dead woman doesn't feature. Yes, it is usually a woman and she is just a brief glimpse, a blur of green body, and then she is gone, out of the picture, disappearing into the depths of nothingness whence she came. I think the principal characters in the television series, deep down, are impressed by the killer, by his will power, by the Napoleon flair with which he vanishes into the night with no trace left behind. What can the dead woman offer? Nothing. And anyway she has nothing to say.

Valle came up to Stockholm and there he stayed. After Havsmon he had gone to Hjo and after Hjo to Jämtland, where he lived for a while when he was little, and after that he lived in Mora and eventually in Södertälje. When he ran away from Södertälje, it was only a few months before his eighteenth birthday. So they let him go his own way and he rented a subleased apartment that they paid for. Then he must have lost that place, because the next time I see him he is sleeping in a doorway. The stone floor is so cold against his face, against his soft, warm cheek, but lying there, drifting within himself, he doesn't feel it; he senses nothing of the world around him, has only the embrace of absence inside rocking him gently to sleep in the wind. He sleeps in stairwells just like his mother, but I have the impression it is harsher now, more dangerous, or maybe it only seems that way because my child is the one sleeping there now. I don't remember being afraid myself, I felt free and invincible when I slept outdoors; I thought I had found a way to cheat the system, to charge along outside time and society, like an animal, not imprisoned inside a cage but unconfined, whilst the rest of the world was kept captive behind its bars. Well, you know where that freedom took me. And now I am afraid when I look at my child.

It is obvious Valle was drawn into my world. At first I was secretly glad, flattering myself that he went there to search for me, but it hurts when I see him waiting for a dealer to come and give him the promised land that evaporates so rapidly. He looks so small, so slender, in his hoodie and bomber jacket, like a child waiting for his parents to take him to the cinema. But I assume he must see what is in my world, as if a hidden trail lies within him that he has to follow, an instinct. Skinny legs in black denim disappearing into a pair of trainers. His hands deep in his pockets, his shoulders hunched, as they are all the time, as if he is always slightly cold; and his wary watchfulness. He has that chemical, unnatural air about him now, as though he isn't human but belongs to an army of the dead. It works as fast on Valle as it did on me; the heroin seizes you with a force greater than any other and it refuses to let go. Though that last bit isn't true; it is you who won't let go of the heroin. I still love the word, but no longer feel the physical manifestation the word produced, the inner rush.

I watch him as he sits on the sofa with a needle in his hand and a flex wound round his arm. Lying beside him are a girl and a boy, knocked out, already half-asleep, smiling. And when I see him sink backwards and throw back his head, suffused as he is now with the great namelessness, I see that this is paradise, this is the paradise on offer to people. I reach out to touch him, his head resting on the other boy's shoulder, almost affectionately, but they have already forgotten one another, and I am the one always forgetting I don't have any hands. And now I see how close it comes each time, death sweeping across the room, its big fist ready to snatch one of them at any moment. Should I hope for it to be over quickly? Should I hope for a grave for my child? What should I hope for?

*

I look away again and when I do I see Solveig and she seems to be forever suffused in a glow. That is why I named her Solveig, so that she should have her own inner sun that would always shine on her when we were there no more. Shane and I decided on the name together, before the thought of giving her away entered my mind. Then I found out her name doesn't even mean sun; it was Raksha who discovered it in a crossword clue, that it means the one who fights. That may be true, and the whole fighting thing might be a good idea, but Raksha could equally have made a mistake, and as far as I am concerned, it still means sunlight. Whatever the reason, Solveig goes through life as though she was never left a changeling in the forest, as if nothing could ever damage her. Do you know where she has got that security from? From me. I gave her away so that she should walk free. If she had stayed with me she would never have started at university; I have always been afraid of those people, in their towers. But Solveig walks through the ancient university buildings with her head held high, a special kind of pride surrounding her, and even from afar you can see that she likes herself. That is another thing I couldn't have given her; from me would have come shame and silence. She sits for days on end in the reading room of the huge library in Uppsala. It looks like an old museum, from the outside like a palace, and some of the books are the size of a child's coffin. The mere name of the library makes me nervous. Carolina Rediviva in gold letters over the entrance. But Solveig moves around so easily in that world. As she seems to do in all worlds, as if ignorant of rules and boundaries, or just pretending she can't see them. Like the fact that she has a girlfriend now. Called Clara. I have heard Solveig call her name.

*

Clara always wears a black leather jacket, even inside the library, and she has febrile eyes, eyes that I see are to fall in love with, their intensity and lustre like pure honey. It is cold in their world now, late November, the trees are bare and the leaves lie stiff and frosty on the ground and I watch Solveig and Clara standing under a tree in Slottsparken, kissing, heedless of the cold around them. Breath steams from their mouths, and all the time Solveig's hands are moving under Clara's jumper. Vaguely I remember that touch of soft skin beneath my hands.

I wanted to bathe in Shane's gaze for ever. But our love was like a stagnant pool of stale, sick water. We were bound together by invisible cords and in the end all we were capable of was wounding each other.

"But at least we did our best," he whispers across time and all the noises of the forest, past death.

"Do you really think so?"

"Yes . . ."

"In that case, Shane, our best was lousy."

He laughs gently. "At any rate, the best thing we did was have Valle and Solveig."

"Wrong again, Shane. Having the children was the most appalling thing of all."

"I'm not afraid of what's ahead. I'm not afraid of anything anymore," Shane said the last time I saw him. It was in the cemetery, I still had the identity wristband on from the maternity ward. We sat between two graves and talked. He was thin, translucent, and he couldn't forgive me for what I had done to us by giving up Solveig. He didn't say as much, but he didn't need to. He didn't look at me, he looked at everything else apart from me, at the crowns of the trees and the clods of earth and clumps of grass he was scratching out of the ground. I wanted to tell him that he had to look at me and that the only thing that could be forgiven was the unforgivable. But perhaps it was a long time since he had looked at me, perhaps I was simply a reminder of all our failures. I asked him if he was going to Istanbul. "Maybe," he said, "maybe not." I dared not ask anything more. He spoke to me as if I were a stranger who had taken a seat beside him. When the silence had lasted a while I walked away. Now I see the scarlet patches on his neck.

I was always going somewhere, always in a hurry; I went with strangers because they were strangers, because they had no notion of who I was. Just as I didn't; there was no-one more of a stranger to me than I was myself. To wake up naked with blood on my thighs in a bike shed on Kocksgatan didn't make me afraid. Only when there was something to fear was I afraid.

"It's because you're a flyer that it's always so fast for you," Shane said tenderly, taking my face in his hands. If there was a good interpretation and a bad, he always chose the good.

"I'm not a flyer," I said. "I'm a drug addict."

Shane saw things no-one else could see; that was why I wanted to be with him and it was why I wanted to be away from him.

"You pretend to belong to this world," he says some time at the beginning, when he still laughs about me forgetting that we were supposed to meet, when I have been gone for days and can't remember where. But I am not good enough at pretending, and something else constantly draws me in, away from him, away from reason. Sometimes I think it is because I see more clearly than everyone else, and I understand more, that I take the drugs. It was the aforesaid angel that unlocked the world for me. Every time it beats its wing inside me, by some topsy-turvy law of nature I fall upwards, against gravity, with the birds and the light. But how can I explain this to Valle? And to Solveig? How can I explain that there is something greater than all the rest, something greater than our life, something greater than Valle's eyes looking at me and believing I will choose him over drugs? I must have been born with a monster in my soul.

I accept they took Valle from me, but I can't accept the way they did it, coming so early in the morning, without notice, snatching him out of our bed. I could have taken him to the social services office myself and sat him down in the playroom and when he was engrossed in one of those toy cars I would have walked away and never gone back. But perhaps they knew I planned to escape with him to Istanbul. Sometimes I think that if they hadn't taken him, we might be there now, Valle and I alone by the Black Sea, winter on its way and the tourists departing, and I would be clean, and there would just be the two of us and nothing of what has happened since would have happened at all. We might have been able to live with Shane's mother. But then I recognise that it is probably as well it ended up the way it did, their stealing him so brutally from my arms, that a single wound is a good thing, a single rupture rending everything apart. So that for the rest of his life he knows I would never have willingly given him up. Not how it was with Solveig; I handed her over, like a parcel.

One day I could stand normality no longer and that was when I crossed over to the other side. It was like walking through a glass wall that smashed soundlessly into a thousand pieces. I stood in a rain of broken glass with my first syringe in my hand and if I could, I would tell you how beautiful it was, as if all things were illuminated from within. Once it has been within reach, there is no way back. You can never return to the earlier world, the one that was there before, even if there were a previous world to which you could return. For me it was never about that. And it wasn't about the physical experience, nor the abstinence, but there is a total stillness and clarity that you can't live without once it is revealed. The world outside has been emptied of meaning, and you begin to understand that it has always been that way, it is raw, ugly, unjust. No-one tells the truth about it, but that is unsurprising, because no-one tells the truth about anything else either.

But now I was lying in the mud by the little lake with a human shadow over me. The trees bent their huge, dark crowns to the lake. I had always thought they bowed their delicate necks over the water in prayer and finally, helplessly, were drawn down, driven by thirst towards death. A hundred years might pass before they drowned, but slowly, imperceptibly, they were on their way. Never in my entire life had I begged anyone for anything; I had never bowed down, like the trees by that lake, to anyone. Instead I had been smashed like a withered branch. I thought of the angel's wings I once believed were mine. But there were no angels, and a darkness enshrouded my vision, and I died.

He leaned over my dead body, which was lying like a shadow on the earth, a puddle of human scraps in blood-soaked shreds of clothing. His face was unmoving, frozen like the world around us, and my head looked so large lying there, as if it belonged to an animal.

"I only wanted to be with you," he whispered to what moments ago had been me.

Time must have flown in Valle's world for he looks so different now. He is bigger, as if he has grown several sizes since the last time I saw him. I couldn't believe it at first, but he has actually given up drugs and as a result that unnatural look he had has disappeared. It is something of a mystery, as he hasn't become religious, he hasn't been in rehab, hasn't fallen in love and I don't think he has suffered a lightning strike to the head; he has simply stopped, and his life is calm. Perhaps the physical exercise has saved him; he works out for several hours a day. At first I thought all those muscles looked odd, as though he were wearing a suit of armour under his clothes, but I suppose it makes him feel invincible. In that case, it is a good thing, if he considers himself more whole, and if he knows he can defend himself. Now that I have grown used to it, I like watching him; he is changed, but still the same, and his skin is glowing and alive, his eyes are as clear now as they were when he was a child. But sometimes I think his life seems so bare and lonely and I am more anxious for him now that he is clean and no longer has something to protect him; and I can't help wishing him the gentle veils of heroin and a single mission that fills the world.

He looks like Shane did at that age and I am almost embarrassed when I see him, as if I am gazing at Shane again. I was so deeply in love with Shane, but falling in love is quite difficult to understand from eternity's perspective and here it is incomprehensible that the tiny reverberation sounding through your body when reason leaves it can have such massive consequences.

Valle looks very much alone walking between job and gym and the little apartment and then sitting the whole evening in the ice-blue glare of the computer screen. And that is life, getting up in the morning, getting dressed, working to earn some money, and then coming home and having something to eat and letting your soul be sucked in by a television or a computer. What else would you do? There is still a silence around him, and it seems that with each year it increases. Sometimes a girl will arrive on the scene and stay for a while, but then she disappears and Valle flies off on a new trip. Always travelling alone. He has a tough job in telesales, but he can handle it; he works incessantly and he gives his all in every telephone call, a place where he isn't afraid to speak. When he has free time, off he goes again; he is good at saving money and he has already been around the world several times and he never looks happier than in that moment when the engines roar and the plane is hauled into the sky as though by some mighty force. I often think about all he has seen on his journeys, the things imprinted on his eye. The Inca Empire. Beirut. The seas off Alaska. The cities in South Africa. The skyline in Shanghai.

Thousands of planes are suspended around the globe, looking from a distance as though they are crawling, when in fact they are streaking along. From above they look like lanterns floating on water. Valle is sitting on one of those aeroplanes right now; I don't know where he is going, but the plane is moving eastward and in the cool of the cabin with the sun shining in through the window and a grey Moscow lying below, he is half asleep. He loves nothing more than flying, as much now as he did that very first time at the age of two when we went to Istanbul, and he spent the entire flight standing stock-still in the seat by the window, staring out.

"What can you see?" Shane asked from the next seat, a protective arm around him so that he wouldn't fall off if the plane were to make a sudden lurch. I thought: Why do we have to return to earth? Why can't we stay up here forever?

"The first time I saw you I knew I wanted to have a child with you," Shane says. It was so weird, we met and ten minutes later we were sitting in a bed under an open window; we had said nothing to each other, just left together. A party at which neither of us knew anyone. Rather like our entire life, a giant party where neither of us actually knew anyone. We walked away to that room with the windows in the roof, the one he used to borrow from a lady in Mosebacke with a view over the whole city where you could always see the sky. We didn't sleep together that first time, we just sat all night looking at one another. It was a long time before we did. It felt as though we had just arrived in the world, we were newborn, like nascent stars at their most vulnerable, material from stellar explosions reforming. But I would never say that to Shane. There are things you cannot say. I don't think I ever said I loved him.

"But you don't know anything about me," he says a little later, when night has returned. We haven't turned on any of the lights; it is easier to talk when we can't see each other. His voice is as naked as a fluorescent tube in the dark.

"Maybe not, but I know I like the person I become when I'm with you."

"And who do you become?"

"I become no-one."

*

The sun was on its way back after night-time, a soft, downy light rising from below, from the ground and the trees, the way it does on certain nights in early summer, when in a burst it starts to flood the world. When I saw my reflection in a toilet mirror in McDonald's, streaks of mascara had run down my face, like black tears; though I wasn't sad, I was happy. I had made myself up to look dangerous.

"You're sweet," Shane said.

"Come on," I said, and we took the metro to the end of the line.

"What if things are happening too fast for us?" Shane asks. I don't think things are moving fast enough. I have always wanted to do everything fast. Love, do my first syringe, have a baby, die.

At night for the first few weeks after we found out I was pregnant with Valle, we lay in a bath in the Hotel Admiral until the water grew cold. On the surface around us floated strands of hair, soap residue, particles of food, semen. Shane had said he wanted us to give up drugs now. "Yes," I said. It was obvious we ought to quit, we ought to quit no matter what, but it was something people said, not something we really meant. But this time he did mean it; he said he would bind me by my hands and feet if I tried to leave. So those first few weeks we were clean, for the first time since we had been together, and wide awake with the harrowing thirst in our blood. Through a window in the bathroom we saw the little band of darkness that was night at this time of year, the dark striation drawing in across our part of the planet only to withdraw at once. All I could think about was the fierce desire as the dark liquid was forced out of the syringe into my blood and spiralled through my body until it met the very source of life. When we slept together it used to feel as though Shane was making love to my naked heart. And now – no feeling at all.

From here I see everything so clearly, from here I see all the twists and turns. One night some time later, when we felt slightly better, I left the Admiral, going out without knowing why. We had celebrated Shane's birthday that night in the window.

"What do you wish for?" I had asked him as we sat in the light of the candle on the Black Forest gateau we had pinched.

"You," Shane said. "I'll never wish for anything else if I can be with you."

"You have me already," I said. "You have to wish for something else. Something nigh on impossible."

His eyes glistened. He didn't look at me when he spoke.

"Every time I go to sleep I'm scared you'll be gone when I wake up."

"Me too," I said, because I was as scared as he was that I would leave. At first he had tied me to the bed, but now he didn't. We weren't sick anymore. The rope lay coiled up by the window.

"But do you need me at all?" he asked.

"If you only knew how much I need you. I would be an angel without you."

After he had fallen asleep I went out and came back with a silver packet. On the metro it gleamed so brightly in my bag I thought everyone could see it. I lay down on the bed and floated away. I had got into the first car that stopped, without checking to see who was sitting inside. When I lay on my stomach on the backseat with a man on top of me who wasn't Shane, I thought I would die, actually die, but I didn't. I stood up and walked back along the narrow wooden bridge over the water past the National Museum and the Grand Hotel, and on through Kungsträdgården to Sergels Torg.

Valle was born and I recognised that we were on the lowest rung over the abyss and that below us was only a gaping black gorge of nothingness. When we left Danderyd Hospital I was afraid they would stop us, but they didn't. We ran across the car park with Valle in the carry-cot, like thieves. He was so sweet with the creases round his eyes. He didn't need to be sweet; it was enough that he existed, was our child. Shane had said he wanted to protect me from all that filled me with fear, from the demons and vampires flocking around us as we lay on the grass in Berzelii Park the first summer after Valle had arrived. We were contained in the boundless radiance of baby-hood, in a dome of sunshine and sky under the trees with the little boy between us as proof that we would never forget one another now; and I think he really tried, he did his utmost to shield me, but he could never save me from myself.

I wish I could say I did all I could to protect Valle, but it isn't true. When he was newborn I thought I would kill myself if I failed to keep him safe, and it was easy not to take anything for the first few weeks; Shane and I were basking in the endless glow there is around a baby. But after a while it started to hurt when I looked at him because he was so defenceless, his little mouth and wide-open eyes seeking me out with such trust; I was terrified that he was dependent on me to survive. It was as if, suddenly, I saw us from the outside, a panoramic picture of us walking under that vast sky with him in the buggy; and

I could see how fragile it all was, how the black birds of doom were circling above our small apartment on Sockenplan, how ridiculous it was of me to believe I could do this. So one day when Shane came home I was sitting with a syringe in my arm, and the moment he opened the door, I pressed it in. Shane's face went white, he stopped in his tracks and just looked at me as I let the wave take me and its force fling me into another world as it always did. He carefully took Valle from my arms and retreated to the bedroom with him. I think in my mind it was up to him to take care of Valle now, so that I could let go for a while, but after a few weeks we were both shooting up. At first – it was later that same evening – I promised I wouldn't take any more, but my one relapse had scratched the fragile surface on which our lives played out and without voicing our intention, we started again. At first only a little, and then as much as before. And later even more than before, because we couldn't face what we were doing to Valle. People say that you can't choose to die if you have a child. But you want to die precisely because you have an innocent little child. Children are the mirrors of death; you see yourself in their eyes, grotesquely magnified. You see yourself succumb, that it is inevitable, that you do them harm. You see it is all your own fault.

Shane made me stop breast-feeding that day, announcing that was the way it would be from now on, and I didn't dare argue. Perhaps everything would have been different if I had been able to carry on. Breast-feeding a baby was the best thing that ever happened to me. When I took him away from my breast the last time, something inside me shattered, not that I blame anyone other than myself, but nevertheless I want to explain that something broke, I even heard it, a strange crunching sound deep inside my body. And yet for the next three years we would fight to keep him. Why? When we could have let go there and then and allowed him to be free of us.

Why should you tell the truth when it is so easy to leave things as they are? It is something I constantly ask myself. But I realise I haven't been alone in all the lies. Lying is part of human nature, an ability refined by evolution. You have to presume that people lie, not the contrary. But I would like to tell the truth. For Valle's sake. The notion of doing the right thing for once, even though it is too late.

Nanna dropped by from time to time. She lay beside me on the bed with her big books. Stoned and beautiful in her sunglasses despite it being winter. Outside, the snow fell soundlessly and she read aloud to me from a book about snow. Her books were always on the theme of snow.

"This is the end," I said after she had closed the book.

"No," she said, "this is the beginning. We have a little baby. We have to be stronger than we are now."

She used to have conversations with Valle when he was inside me; it felt pretty silly, but good, and Nanna always knew what to say. She talked about herself, and sometimes she talked about me as if I wasn't there.

"Hi, little person," she said to my stomach, patting it. When she spoke I saw thousands of shadows behind her head, shadows of all of those she had driven away with into the night, the ones we made a living from. She said she would take care of the baby should anything happen to me, she would be there come what may. Then she disappeared again. There was no-one who could make herself as invisible as she could when she wanted to.

"I'm here," she said every time she appeared, only to vanish once more. When she hid behind her hair she looked like a tiny animal.

"Can't you see the sky?"

"No," I said; his large head was in the way and all I could see was him. Thunderstorm eyes staring at me. Wide with lust, icy with loathing. The passage of an instant and a thousand years there in the forest. I could feel my heart, filling with blood and emptying of blood and then filling with blood again, I saw my arms drop to the ground, and what had been my body was still. If I could do it all again, would I go with him? I fear that I would. This moment was the culmination of a thousand and one other moments. And the silver packet twinkled in his hand.

His pale grey eyes are flecked under the vaulted lids; he has a graceful, almost subtle way of moving, like a dancer, with an elegance to all his movements, and he doesn't look dangerous. And as for his face, it is transfigured before me, the leaden eyes suddenly filled with blackness, an eclipse of the eye, the chill of death pouring from his soul. Desire, pure and raw. When he looks at me his stare is so intense it burns my skin. He touches my breast, he touches my face, my lips and eyes, and in that stare, lust and hate are forever intertwined. Here am I, naked and cold before him, and he severs my head from my body as if it were an insect's, and for one reeling moment, though my head is disconnected from my body, my eyes are still alive and for a few split seconds I do indeed see the sky, before it burns out and the light disappears and cold water bubbles in, between my skull and brain.

Did I really think he would kill me? Yes, maybe I did, but I didn't think it would be the end; I believed all along I would return, as someone else, that I would be forgiven. Forgiven for what? I don't know, simply forgiven. For being born, for existing in the world. Killed, and then brought back. Lost. Liberated.

It is eight thousand metres as the crow flies from Haga Park to Hägersten where my body was found, twelve thousand by car via the motorway. Maggots, some of them still chrysalids, are crawling around me. The odd fly, green. Lethargic, barely moving. That first autumn people everywhere are saying it was someone with a head for maths who murdered me. A hunter or a dancer. A scientist or an architect. To which I could add the judge I slept with towards the end; he used to hunt in the forests outside Uppsala, but maybe he never told the police that? As far as I am concerned, it makes no difference who did it, who is guilty of my death, I mean. If the gods were put on trial, they would all be acquitted, and I have always known I would die young. And I am like Snow White, afraid of nothing, not of huntsmen or forests or murderers. My problem is that I didn't want to be saved.

All I know is this: if I had managed to escape, I would have had nowhere to go, and if I had been able to say who he was, if my tongue hadn't been cut out and my mouth filled with earth, no-one would have believed me. So what does it matter who did it? I got into his car and we drove past the high-rise buildings and the fields and on into the green landscape and that was the last time I saw the city.

Thus it is: suddenly you are holding a dead girl in your arms, cold and white as marble, despite the fact you thought you would simply drive her back to the city afterwards and drop her off in Kungsträdgården and see her disappear between the overblown cherry trees. For something else took over, from nowhere, without warning, like a wave rising inside you, and once there it obliterated all else, flooding the world in a gruesome black ooze of water; you couldn't find a way to withstand it, and nor perhaps did you want to. You were filled with a godlike strength, controlling life and death, heaven and earth. Immortal. Invincible. This demon, for it is a demon and a god of sorts that takes up residence in humans, has lived in him for many years and only shown itself from time to time, the shadow brother or furious genie someone has accidentally let out of a bottle. Afterwards it seems to him it was all a dream. But he can't take anything from that dream, he can't keep the dead girl, he has to part with her in the forest. He will always remember me with tenderness. Yes, tenderness.

In any event, now we are in the forest by the thousand-year-old lake and an organ that must be my womb lies in his hand, grey and glistening and bloody. It looks as though it weighs so little, no more than a hen's egg.

I could have asked:

"Will we come back again? Can you promise me that I'll come back to my children?"

But I had no children to come back to; there was just me and that city and its architecture of cruelty.

The same goes for Eurydice. She has already been raped by the gods and for her it is all too late. It isn't that Orpheus wasn't permitted to turn his head and look at her, she couldn't care less about that, it is simply that she must have a pretext for remaining in the underworld. You need an excuse for choosing darkness.

Shortly after I had met Shane we went into the city one evening to buy shoes, and I went off for two weeks. I was going back to him the entire time, to everyone I met during that period I would say I was going home, and it was the first time in my life I had felt like that, that I actually was going home. "I'm going home," I said to anyone who asked, and I was so tremendously happy when I said it. But for all that, I didn't go home.

Solveig must have persuaded Clara to go with her from Uppsala to Stockholm, where she is living now, because every time I see Solveig, Clara is around. She is still constantly in that leather jacket, indoors as well, and her eyes are just as intense when she looks at Solveig, filled with light and loving kindness. Solveig has started wearing a suit, and shiny shoes and a coat from the NK department store. Every day she enters one of those sky-blue buildings next to the Museum of Natural History and stays inside for hours. "Time is movement," she says. Movement is reality. Maybe so. Nothing here moves; it is all in a state of perpetual doldrums.

When Solveig and Clara talk about their lives, it sounds as though their words are coming from a book. They never speak about me, and nor does Valle, when he speaks at all, perhaps because they don't know much about me. Solveig knows only what she has been told. She knows that I am dead, she knows that I was an addict and that she was taken into care at a very young age.

But one day she goes into a record office and looks everything up. She spends an entire day in the Stockholm City Archives on Kungsholmen and reads everything there is to be read about us. I see her sitting alone under the little green lamp in the dark reading room. Next to her are the nine cardboard boxes in which all the details of our lives can be found, the police investigations as well as the reports from social services.

She stares for a long time at the small passport photograph of me affixed to the first page, the photo that was in all the newspapers. The one with the frizzy hair I had at the end, and where my eyes look harder and deeper than before. I look straight into the camera's flash, but you can see that I am already far away, distant and unhappy. Maybe she recognises my eyes and her own narrow face, covered with freckles. The photo was taken a few months after her birth, in the spring. It was for a new passport so that I could follow Shane to Istanbul, which was where I thought he was, but by the time the passport arrived I was already inside those suitcases, stinking to high heaven.

She stares at length at the photograph, large, round tears rolling from her eyes, each one making a tiny sound as it plops onto the table. It is here in the underground corridors of Kungsklippan that I become her mother for the first time, when she sees the little black and white passport photograph taped onto a stencilled sheet. It is when she reaches the end of the story, where it says that, even before she was born, we asked them to take her. By then she has already seen the sketches and photographs of my dead body in pieces. In the documents it states that we presented ourselves five months into the pregnancy, it states that we wouldn't accept any of the assistance they offered us and that we wanted to sign the papers as quickly as possible. It doesn't say that this was the only thing we had to give her, that it was the only thing of value we had to offer, a life without us; it doesn't say that we were in such a hurry because we were afraid we would change our minds. It does say she has a brother, named Valentino, born three years before she was.

*

An odour of lake and forest emanates in waves from the old documents and I can see she feels nauseous now; she has her hand over her mouth and her brow is glistening with perspiration, her face grey. I wonder why Clara isn't with her. But she is not in the city, I realise, for when Solveig calls her and weeps into her phone, she can't come, but her voice is tender and close. And I don't think this is me, I would never hurt Solveig, but suddenly there is a trickle of dark, slimy water between her feet and a roar from deep inside the building. And now the black water surges along the corridors, it rises in the reading room with the green lamps, dark and full of earth and ash, and Solveig drops all the papers and runs, up, towards the light. The documents once written about us are carried away in the river of black. Outside in the light she sits down. She opens her hand and in it is the photograph of me.

Are you still listening? It doesn't matter if you aren't, I long since gave up caring whether anyone heard what I said. In my experience most people are so self-absorbed they find it hard to hear anything other than their own thoughts. You see impatience squirming through them like a snake when it isn't their turn to speak, and then you want to come to their rescue and let them carry on. But there are exceptions, those who quieten when they hear another voice, like Shane, and Nanna.

Many of those I met on Herkulesgatan were there to talk. That was the most trying aspect, it was easier with the ones who just wanted to get it done and didn't drag things out; I felt sullied by their words. Some of them thought they were finally *sub rosa* and began their confession as soon as the car door slammed shut. My job might just as well have been that of a psychologist or a priest. You get slightly better at listening when you are dead, because you hear everything then. When you have time to replay all your conversations, you hear the nuances in what was once said and you miss nothing, which is awful too, as it is too late by far. But if this is the penalty, all this listening and rewinding, then what is the crime? I will never know.

I don't recognise the world I grew up in; it all looks so different, people moving in a different way, more diffidently, more self-consciously, as if great mirrors were held in front of them.

They all say everything is worse, but maybe it is also marginally better. It must be the disappointment of soaring expectations that clouds their view; it is always best to assume nothing. Or perhaps it is the same old raw human spirit masquerading as the future that blinds me. The exhibitionists are still there anyway, standing in the tunnels with their trousers open, but as they only expose themselves to children, adults of every new generation believe they are a thing of the past. Most of the shops have moved away from Herkulesgatan down into a shadow world, an old-fashioned high street shop being almost impossible to imagine now, like mediaeval cripples earning money from their misfortune. No, it hasn't completely disappeared, but it is smaller and mostly frequented by undocumented women, the ones with less than nothing. But really everything is the same, just new places and new variations on the old theme.

At the spot where our house once stood I watch the river, its emerald-green water flowing along, the black water lilies reaching for the surface as I once reached for Raksha. There have been so many times I have thought I should stay away, not disturb anyone, leave Valle and Solveig to become the people they will become without me. Hanging in the little chantry in the church by the river is the same Jesus as when I was a child. I used to look into his kind eyes, the only gaze I wasn't afraid to meet. He too had made a mess of things and his father must have been angry with him as well, because he left him hanging there, bleeding and forlorn.

One day Valle was standing on a chair with a rope around his neck. His eyes were as steady as glass, a film of fever on his face, and he looked utterly calm, still, as though suspended in a kind of serenity. I know how that serenity feels. The sun shone outside his window, which was slightly open, and a pale winter light was streaming into the room. Things lay all over the floor, clothes, dirty plates, pizza boxes. The rope was strong, I could see, and I stayed close beside him without knowing what I ought to do. It didn't matter, there was nothing I could do anyway. He was somewhere else, in another world. Soon he would be far from here.

"Mamma," he said plainly, into the room. Then he lifted up his feet, but he didn't kick the chair away. I heard his rattling breaths, as if they were my own, but I couldn't do anything. The rope tightened and he stopped breathing. I shouted, but my voice made no sound. I tried to pull him down, but I had no hands. I tried to hold on to him and force the rope out of his hands, but I had no earthly power, nor power of any other kind. I saw my child dying in front of me and the world grew still, the remains of the world that I was in, the remains of light.

Why shouldn't he kick the stool away and be free? I knew how lonely he was, knew how long he had struggled, and so much in his life had turned out fine now, without being *good*. Should he live for me to be able to drop in on him from time to time and gaze at his handsome face? I thought: If he can just get through the next few seconds, nothing will ever hurt him again. I imagined him coming to me, although I know it doesn't work like that. The word "peace" passed through my thoughts. And I remembered he loved flying. So I whispered to him, told him he should fly away, fly out of time. I don't know if that was why he suddenly managed to wrench off the rope and he fell to the floor. His body trembled with weeping, he retched and coughed, and from above it looked as though someone had taken hold of him and was shaking him. And then he grew still. Sunlight filled the room, a rainbow arced in the sky between the high-rise buildings, and I let him be alone. You might think I made that up about the rainbow, but I didn't. I may have invented some tiny detail in the story, but the rainbow outside Valle's window that morning, that bit is true.

I didn't think I would dare look in on him again after the episode with the rope; I was sure I would find him in the morgue, as cold as snow. But one day I couldn't stop myself taking a little peep, and when I did, there he was, sitting at a café in the sun with Solveig. Solveig!

The first spring sunshine had arrived and Solveig was wearing a big yellow quilted jacket. Valle appeared to be so happy, almost carefree, his eyes bright and full of light, and he looked straight at Solveig without lowering his gaze. It can't have been the first time they had seen one another, they must have met before, because I noticed they already knew each other and were talking about things they had clearly spoken about earlier. Solveig must have gone back to the social services and asked them to give her his name, and because Solveig is Solveig and possesses the charm of words, she must have left the office with his name in her pocket and then one day stood at his door and told him she was his sister. And now they were sitting there, she with her Elvis haircut and he with the enigmatic little topknot on his head that made him look like Little My. They laughed a lot and I laughed too, though I made no sound. I had never heard him say so much, words spilling out of him like pearls. And now that I saw Valle and Solveig together, I could see their likeness to Raksha and Ivan, and in their happy faces I saw glimmers of the people who had once been my parents, like faint eddies in a pool. I was struck by a new and violent sense of loss at the unexpected realisation I was missing myself, and I had to look away for a moment.

She had been so scared, Solveig said, that they would be alike, and scared that they wouldn't be in the least alike. But most of all she was scared that he would shut the door in her face when he saw her.

"But I've never been happier in my entire life," Valle said.

"Did you realise who I was?"

"At once."

"Even though you didn't know I existed?"

"That's my little sister, I thought."

Valle worked at Arlanda now, selling perfume and cosmetics in a glossy mirrored tax-free shop where he could see the aeroplanes take off. He must already have told Solveig he used to take drugs, for now she asked:

"Why did you stop?"

"I don't know. I just did."

And he said he had always known he would take his own life, ever since he was a child, alone in the forest with his knives and the dogs; it was the thing of which he was most certain, that he would die young.

"Why are you telling me this?" Solveig said.

"So you're not afraid."

"But I am afraid."

They sat in silence for a while.

"What keeps you here?" Solveig finally asked.

"I don't know. I just don't seem to be able to get away. And I'm frightened I would be reborn as something even worse."

"OK," Solveig said.

"OK?"

She looked at him and then said:

"I'm not going to try to stop you if you really don't want to stay, but obviously, I'd be really happy if you did stick around."

Part of me can't wait for humankind to perish as a species. It is a childlike notion, that the world should have shuddered to a stop the moment I breathed my last, when he strangled me in the forest. But I know that only my world stopped, your world sped on without me. Life was what it was, and so was death.

Another part of me wants everything to carry on, for humanity to have another chance, just as I sometimes wish for another chance myself; but those thoughts lead nowhere, only down into the darkness. Still, I sometimes send a prayer into the nothingness, even though I know there is only the void of the spinning solar system and the cold chalky light of the Milky Way. I pray for Raksha and Ivan and I pray for Solveig and Valle. *Keep these people in the light. Guard them from evil forces.* Sometimes I fear I might accidentally be worshipping those evil forces.

One day I will let go and reel back into the nothingness whence I came. I watch Raksha for hours and wish she would utter my name; I need to know that I still exist within her, but she has no-one to whom she could say it. She has a coffee with Sylvia every Sunday and sometimes she cuts her hair. That is the only time she speaks to anyone, but she never mentions us. Not me, not Eskil.

She still has two children, just as I do, for you always have your children, and death can't change that, neither for me nor her. You can't stop being a mother, no matter how much you might try to break free. For a while she had Ivan, when he reappeared after my death, but then he left and now she has only Sylvia. Sylvia, with her dandelion hair, who chatters on into the air about nothing as Raksha sits listening, hands on her knee. My longing to return is fading, the sense of loss subsiding; here there is only the wind and the faint scent of eternity and oblivion. When I look at the people I have left behind, they too are strangers.

Sometimes I think I would like to ask Raksha what she meant when she said she couldn't be my mother any longer.

"But how could I say anything so foolish? Of course you were my child," she might mumble as she lies half asleep in the bath and lets a sleeping pill disperse inside her.

"So it was just that you couldn't cope any longer, with being my mother?"

"But obviously I wanted to be your mother. That's all I've ever wanted."

"But that's what you said."

"Yes, but we say a lot of things we don't really mean. Stupid to go through life believing something like that. I was in the depths. Literally in the darkest depths of the damned river. You shouldn't believe everything you hear."

"But you weren't happy before that either."

"Wasn't I? No, maybe I wasn't. Some people will never really be happy. But you can't be as precise and pernickety about words as you are. That way disaster lies."

"My disaster has already happened, Mamma."

You are eternally joined to the person who killed you and getting used to that is the hardest part. To see into the people you love is one thing, but to see into the one who murdered you is something else entirely. You have to face your own death, over and over. For a while I wondered how he could carry on living with me on his conscience, but not anymore. The human capacity for suppression is infinite; memory is only one part of the psyche and the task of the organism is to rearrange memory to prevent the person going under. A long time ago I considered revenge, it smouldered inside me; but the feeling is no longer there, and even if it were, it isn't feasible.

Inside him is a barren, desolate wasteland, and yet he has that particular agility of so many madmen; something about him seems entirely open and candid and he readily connects with people. Maybe he doesn't radiate warmth, but he has a presence, an intensity, something that intimates he is rather different. But no-one would think he was dangerous. And if the images of death ever surface inside him, just before he falls asleep or just after he has opened his eyes in the morning, they are torn, fragmented, out of context. It is like a film he might have seen in the cinema long ago. I believe he expends a great deal of energy keeping me at a distance and in the end there is only a narrow shred remaining on which to live; his life diminishes until there is almost nothing left. In recent years he has withdrawn, he no longer stands at the fence chatting to the neighbours and not long ago his wife moved out. I heard her say it felt as though she loved an empty shell.

From here I see myself from the outside, like a photograph, and time and time again I see myself with Valle, sitting at a plastic table in Burger King waiting for a pimp or a dealer. When I look now I see he has fallen asleep in my arms. It is just after midnight and he has dark shadows under his eyes. Why don't I go home? Why do I just sit and let time go by? I know that in the end they will come and take him if I don't change. Is that what I want? Is that what I wanted all along? I can't make sense of it any other way, because I let it happen.

BREATH

Shane was in Istanbul again, Valle would soon be three and I didn't know how long we were going to be on our own, so Valle and I wandered around the city together. We sat in Kungsträdgården and looked at the pink trees that had just burst into bloom. Valle was no longer a baby, he was a miniature person, sitting there, looking at me. Sometimes he reached out his hand to catch the tiny petals swirling in the air like snow. I longed for Shane to ring, but when he did, I didn't know what to say. When I think of our life now, it seems as though it was all about standing in separate telephone boxes trying to get hold of one another. The feeling of suffocation when we couldn't. And then when we did hear the other's voice, when it was suddenly so close and meant everything in the world, then we had nothing to say.

"Where have you been?" he shouted from an infinite distance.

"Only here."

"Can I speak to Valle?"

"Not at the moment."

"He's there, isn't he?"

"Yes, where else would he be?"

One day we were offered the chance to live at Harry's on Floragatan. I had lived there before and Shane and I had been there often while we were expecting Valle. Harry had two massive grey dogs, Great Danes, and he always wanted people around him. He had nothing else to spend all his money on and someone off the street was always living there. Many was the day I lay on his huge bed watching the flicker of the television. There was the constant sound of voices elsewhere in the apartment where I was languishing in a haze on the bed, under which was a pharmacy fit for a king, everything you could possibly want. I think all that medication had something to do with his job.

This city is full of men in need of company and not all of them are after sex; many daren't, they are too old, too scared, or it is something else, they want a thrashing or to be rocked like a baby. Sometimes Harry asked me to watch over him when he wrapped himself inside his plastic bags and masturbated. When he came I had to pull off the bag, quickly, so he didn't suffocate, but I never had to touch him, he did that himself. I tried it too a few times. When the air supply is choked, it creates a rush in the body like heroin, but it is faster and harder, and more dangerous, I think. I didn't ever feel anything sexual, it was more existential for me, hanging for a second on the edge. From time to time he would get girls to do things with the dogs, but not me. I would never have done it. That is a lie. I would have done anything for access to his chemist's shop. He just never asked.

We stay there for weeks. Valle runs in and out of all the doors, delighted with the vast halls after being used to our little two-roomer. We play with the dogs and sometimes he is allowed to take them out with Harry to Humlegården. Most of the time I lie half asleep under a radiator. I keep thinking we should go home, but we just don't make it, and Valle loves being with the dogs. Do you remember, Valle, how much you loved those huge dogs?

All the lights are on at Harry's around the clock. It is never night-time. From my position lying on the floor underneath the hot radiator I see the towering canine shadows. I am so cold, despite it being warm outside. The treetops rustle in the gentle breeze, the soft tinkle of a thousand tiny bells. In a distant part of the apartment I hear Valle's high-pitched voice and it sounds as though he and Harry are racing from room to room. Valle's squeal, the sound he makes when someone tickles him, and a lower, deeper voice, also exuberant, open. I think of the games we played when I was a child, of being in constant fear of the other children. They always knew what they wanted, they always had a plan, and they had willpower, a desire for something that fuelled them like electricity. Valle was never afraid of anyone, he liked them all.

Nanna with her bleached hair is a silhouette in the bedroom doorway against the fiery radiance of the sunset.

"You've got to get out of here, now."

That evening we leave Harry's.

Nanna pushes Valle in his buggy and takes us down under the ground where no ill can befall us.

"I've been looking everywhere for you."

"We were only here."

"I thought you were dead."

"Here I am," I say, holding out my hands as if I were a gift.

Nanna doesn't laugh. It is a long time since she laughed.

"Where are we going?" I ask instead.

"We're going home."

"But I don't want to go back to Sockenplan."

The metro plunges into the rock above us and I can't hear her reply.

Dirty blankets everywhere and the bundled shapes of people sleeping in the dim ash-yellow light. This is where I have friends, I have Nanna, and she is afraid of no-one, ever. Folk here move slowly, as if under water, and there is no light, only the occasional flash of a torch and the glow of the fires. Someone might get angry, grab someone else by the throat or give them a sudden thump, but it amounts to nothing and is soon over; and no-one hides anything down here, so there is nothing to be afraid of, there are no secrets, no-one is worth more than anyone else, we are all equally worthless, we belong to no-one, we have nothing.

The first time it was Shane and I who lived here, and that was a long time ago, when we had only just met. We slept close to each other by a warm concrete wall and the sound of the metro trains rushing past never stopped. Water ran down the wall, waste water probably, but it was always warm there, like lying next to the sleeping body of a giant, and the sound of the water calmed me. That time I thought we were free, autonomous, because we had nowhere to live. Now I have Valle with me it is so different. If Nanna wasn't here I would leap in front of a train with Valle in my arms.

I watch Valle and Solveig all the time, and all the time they are together again, one always where the other is. Valle stays over at Solveig and Clara's and there he can sleep without nightmares. The summer is warm and they keep all the windows open, and the sky retains a faint blue tinge throughout the night. Valle sleeps on his stomach in the moonlight next to Solveig and Clara, entangled in one another like baby animals in a den, and I think that nothing could hurt them now they are no longer alone in the world. Clara takes photographs with her huge camera and hangs them up all around the apartment, and Valle's eyes are happy as he sits with them in the boundless summer light. Early in the morning, before the city is awake, they go down to Lake Råstasjön. They dive into the dark water and disappear and each time they come up again it makes me dizzy, seeing their wet heads break the smooth black surface as they draw air and summer into their lungs. The dark motionless of the lake water and the relief of drawing breath again. The light piercing your eyes and the world returning. From above, my children's heads look like water lilies, alone in the black sheen of the still water, and from higher up like tiny pinheads, until finally they are invisible and there is just the lake's shiny surface reflecting the clouds. You might suppose it is a dream, a fantasy the dead indulge in to pass the time. In that case, perhaps life was also just a dream.

In the end it is easier to look at the murderer than those you love. It hurts less. I wonder if he is afraid of what is to come, afraid of the flames? I believe he is, even though he has been a confirmed atheist since childhood. He is older now, weaker, and he finds it hard to see. I have watched him fumbling for pieces of furniture in his house to avoid tripping over. Is he imagining a classic hell, with fires and pitchforked demons, women's muffled screams, children's unrelenting cries, a rubbish dump of human remains in searing flames that do not cleanse? Or is it merely a sneaking unease that he will be engulfed in greyness, lose his human form? I could quell his anxiety with the following simple information: the human being is alone in eternity, there is no heaven, no gods, no Father Christmas, we are entirely outside the scrutiny of higher powers. There is no punishment, but neither is there forgiveness. When the end comes, you are alone. You fall headlong into nothing.

I am looking forward to seeing him die. I hope it hurts. I hope he is afraid, as I was. Fear is the worst thing, the hope of escape, before the realisation that you won't. I will be there, wishing him a lonely suffering, on a level with the torment of Jesus.

It was June, early summer, my last.

We sat for a while, gazing out over the misty green landscape and listening to the purr of the engine until he switched off the headlights and turned to me.

"Get out of the car and wait for me," he said, and I got out of the car and waited for him. Then I heard his voice beside me.

"Shall we get going?"

I stepped out into the gentle rain, summer a chamber of damp around me, the trees standing high, their crowns heavy with rain. All the noise had gone. The birds, raindrops, the hum of the engine, the perpetual buzz of electricity cables; the world was silent, soundless. How can anyone be stupid enough to try to hide in a telephone box? That is the kind of question you ask yourself in retrospect. Telephone boxes have disappeared now, but you remember them, don't you? They were everywhere, you stood inside one, drenched, like being in an old jar of formaldehyde at the edge of the forest. He was waiting for me in the car, the headlights illuminating the world of rain around us, and the rest of the world seemed to have been swallowed up by the creeping mist that evening and we really were the only people left on earth. In places the sky was so low, the treetops vanished into the cloud. And didn't

I tell you that I tried to run? I hurled myself out of the telephone box when he came back, I ran into the forest and he came after me and threw me down on the ground and took me like an animal in the mud before he dragged me back to the car.

The mist infiltrates all the hollows and seeps into the ground with the blood from my nose and mouth and all the sounds truly have stopped, the whistle of the storm, the breaking branches, the beat of the rain against my face and the awful screech of the birds, as if the sky has absorbed the world's noise, and one of my eyes must have filled with blood for suddenly half the world is in darkness. Red water rising across the landscape, mounting, though it seems to be trickling down over the trees behind glass. Like human waste, effluent, sliding slowly down the world's protective glass film that has never allowed me through; I have always stood outside, watching life unfold inside. Crawling like an insect on the outside. And now the forest opens out, the trees become sparser and there is the road again, winding through the countryside like a grey streamer. And I must have run in a loop, for now the car is standing in front of me, a cold, alien object in the landscape, belonging in the world of people, shining dimly in the greyish green and yellow of the rain-drenched light. The car door is open like a mouth and he looks at me, standing still as a beast that has already vanquished its prey, still as someone who knows that people like me will always run in circles, and in a few strides he is beside me and drags me down onto the ground and sits on my chest. His clothes are covered in mud and sand, everything is wet, dew and rain and water from the underworld gradually rising below us, the dark water of death, and beneath my shoulders I feel a gentle pull, as if it is the earth that is taking me back and not he who is despatching me. Now he is the giant bird of my childhood, sitting on my chest, pecking out my eyes.

The smell of the lake spreads like an open wound, the same smell that once filled the delivery room, of sludge and seaweed and untainted putrefaction, the inside of the body exposed, the soul laid bare as the flesh it is. He quietens and stares at me with a primordial gaze, lacking all humanity. Have you ever seen such a look? Fixed and cold, a frozen fury, pure instinct.

"You came back to me."

My voice is no more, water and earth are clogging my throat and my lungs are filling with blood. What would I say if I had a voice? What would I say if there was still time? I don't know.

By the time we were back in the car after I had tried to run and the road was growing narrower and the forest encroaching more intensely, I had decided to offer no resistance; I wanted to meet death without begging for mercy, but my body would not be defeated so easily. In the end something else took over and I hit out and screamed for Raksha. But, when his hands squeezed my neck and he raped me, then came the numbness, purling through my veins, bringing stillness, and I was no longer afraid.

I lay on the shore in pieces and there was nothing left to fear. It all happened quickly now, the light disappeared from the sky and it was dark by the lake. He washed his face in the sweet lake water and sat for a moment, staring out across the water and the silhouettes of the fir trees on the other side. Then he dragged the suitcases down the small bank and in them he carefully laid what was left of me. I was a pile of flesh on the grass. I was raw nature, a shapeless bright-red pulp of meat bearing no resemblance to a person, I was the precursor to earth and stardust, one carcass among many. Was this desire in its purest form? To conquer the other person's body?

It is as if the lake sucks in everything that lives; the smooth water absorbs the last of the twilight glow, the flowers and trees are magnetically drawn to its silvery surface, shrubs and saplings lean in its direction, as if bent by a wind. The same applies to the sky, which sees its reflection in the black lake, and to any careless child in summer when the water is smooth and warm. They reach for life, and they meet death.

"My child . . ." Raksha calls from somewhere far, far away. The treetops spin around above and I think they are birch trees; they sound like birches, the faint rustle or swish in the wind, the flickering, fractured light descending through the small green leaves. It is so long since I was in touch with Raksha. I had thought I wanted nothing more from her. No questions, no presents, no telephone calls. But now I wish she could come to this forest outside the world and hold me while I die.

"Is there anyone there? Raksha, are you there? . . . Raksha, I think I've messed myself . . . Are you there, Mamma?"

There is not an awful lot of blood when you cut up dead bodies and he was painstaking and careful, almost tender, when he moved my body around on the shore. He looked like someone who had done it before and he took his time, wasn't rushed by darkness falling and the moon emerging from behind the trees as if someone was shining the icy beam of a giant spotlight on him. And he wouldn't leave a single trace, not a strand of hair or a fragment under my nails.

My head drops onto the wet grass. A gentle rain settles over the little forest and a cold streak of light spreads above the trees when he drives back to the city with me in the boot. The church service is still on the radio but he changes stations, to the news. *The Falkland Islands have just surrendered to Great Britain. The last battle was waged with bayonets and machine guns. A bloody moon rises over Europe.* He arrives at his home, spends a long time washing his hands, face, neck, genitals, he has a shower, washes his hair, vacuums, scrubs, cleans all the windows, falls asleep early between soft clean sheets. It is like an inner renewal.

Many times I had imagined that death didn't want me; it took a taste and spat me out. But in the end it had obviously changed its mind. What can be said about that? It was a shame I couldn't stay alive, but no-one survives life.

We sat beside the angels at the altar in Klara Church and shared a hamburger. Above us was the painting of Jesus when they took him down from the cross. It was night-time and there was only the faint sound of someone asleep between the rows of pews. Valle was sleeping in his buggy next to us. Nanna had a cat with her that she was looking after for someone. It climbed around on the altar for a while before curling up on her knee and falling asleep too.

"You need to go home now," she said.

"I know."

"When it's light, take the metro."

We were silent. I thought I could hear the sound of the candle flames burning around us.

"What about you? Don't you want to come?"

"I'll stay here."

"Sometimes I think he'll never come back," I said.

Nanna pulled the little smile that meant she had already seen it all and she wasn't impressed.

"Yes he will. People always think that when they've left someone."

The cat woke up and stretched. I recalled all the times I had believed Nanna had gone forever and then suddenly she was back on Herkulesgatan, like a wonderful old ghost.

"Sometimes it feels as though you only exist inside me," I said now, "as if you're someone I've invented."

"Sure, but you could have invented something better while you were at it."

"But I think you're the most beautiful thing I could ever have come up with," I said, and her eyes glistened. She lifted the little cat up to her face and kissed its pink nose. The cat shut its eyes.

"Come on. No time to be sentimental now, babe. That won't help either of us."

Shane was back. One day he was simply standing in front of us while we were walking along. He was pale and sunken.

"Hey, mate," he said as he stepped out of our doorway, and he crouched down in front of the buggy. Valle's eyes widened, he cautiously put out his hand and touched Shane's face. He said nothing, just looked intently at his dad, without blinking. Shane lifted him up and held him to his chest and I could see him crying silently into Valle's hair. I didn't ask what he had been doing, I was too proud for that, and nor did he tell me, but I think I understood by then that he was sick.

When Valle had fallen asleep I took my first needle for weeks and it left me unconscious. Now I think it would have been better if I had taken death's hand for once. Instead I dragged myself through light and dark to resurface in the subdued lamplight where Valle lay sleeping in his old cot that was actually too small for him.

"Why doesn't he say anything?" Shane asked after Valle had fallen asleep in my arms. It was the only way to get him to sleep, even though he was too big. Shane had tried to make him say something. Valle looked pleased, but he said nothing, just gazed at Shane with quick bright eyes.

Before, words had come and he talked all the time, a gentle babble pouring out of him, though the words were hard to distinguish. Some individual words were quite clear – doll, lion, doggie, Mamma – but now they had gone.

"We don't talk much," I said.

I believed that words were just a way of hiding things you couldn't bear to know. Without words the world lies before you, naked and true.

Shane had bruises on his chest that hadn't been there before. At night I lay and looked at him while he slept. He was so handsome, the thin, pale skin on his eyelids that always gave him an expression of vulnerability, the hair on his neck curling under the smooth black hair on top. Sometimes he slept so deeply I thought he was dead. "You're alive, aren't you?" I whispered, and felt his ribs. He was breathing, but I could sense he was far away.

That last period we had with Valle was the calmest for us. We took stuff, but not much. It was almost as if we couldn't be bothered. We bathed in Barnhusviken and walked in the warm weather that had arrived in the city despite it only being April. Valle got a dolphin balloon at Gröna Lund that he wouldn't let go, even when he was asleep. We sunbathed in Kungsträdgården and I read aloud from *The Wizard of Oz* in the twilight while Valle fell asleep on Shane's chest. Valle laughed again, but still he said no words. It didn't matter, there wasn't much to say. Other than the three of us belonged together. I remember thinking that was what a family was, people who belonged together.

It was early one morning and the three of us were asleep in the large bed. Valle must have sensed that his present life was about to end, for that night he had come in with us. Quick footsteps across the plastic mat and then he crept under the quilt beside me, his little body made cold by the night. I lay awake while he gradually warmed up beside me, thinking about him still wanting to be in with us, and that night I swore that we would finally go to that home by the sea for mothers and children that had been offered to us, though Shane wouldn't have been able to come with us. But how many times had I had that thought? Valle and I would never go to the sea. In my mind I can still see the picture of us that last night all tangled up together, from just above, as if I were a bird on the ceiling looking down at us. Shane lying behind me, his leg round my waist, his black hair covering his face, Valle curled up under my arm like a little hedgehog.

We were woken by the harsh sound of the doorbell. The room was light. And suddenly it was full of people putting his things into large boxes. The sound of wings was deafening, I couldn't hear what they were saying, and small white feathers filled the air like snow. A pillow had been torn open. By me? By Shane? Not Shane. He just sat and stared at me, a hat pressed to his heart as his only shield, while one of the women picked up his child and carried him out of the room. And now Valle could speak again, calling for me in a tiny, broken voice. "Mamma . . . Mamma . . . Help me, Mamma . . ." Then the door closed and there was silence. As if he had never been there, as if we had never had a child.

It was that night Solveig came to be. We summoned her from the darkness, though we both knew she should have stayed where she was. Unborn, safe, ensnared deep within nothingness. When we made love we did it robotically, like two dolls. The image of Valle quivered between us and the orgasm hurt, as if a baby was bulging out between my legs again and dropping to the floor.

I stood for days on end outside the building that had swallowed up my child. Sometimes I went up to someone and asked:

"When will I get my baby back?"

I was so afraid they would ask which baby I was talking about, but they almost never replied, just hurried through the doors with their handbags pressed to their hips, as if it was their bloody handbags I wanted. Standing there alone, looking at my shadow on the wall, it was as though I had never had a baby boy, never pulled Valle's buggy up and down all the hills in this city. But most of the time I simply stood and watched them. Sometimes I ran up and grabbed at the coat of one of them I knew. Well, I say knew. They knew everything about me, but I knew nothing about them. All they wanted to find out was whether I was high. "Are you high, Kristina?" You're damn right I am, I screamed, kicking out at them. Was that their only question? I had lots of questions. I wanted to say he was better off on the street with me than with strangers, I wanted to say that I was his mother. Sometimes I saw children's shadows at the windows and I heard the trill of their laughter from behind the closed face of the building. One night I threw a stone at a window and scrambled inside, but there were no children; I ran down the empty corridors calling his name. Empty corridors filled with icy silver moonbeams, and room after room filled with the same compassionless silver light. I tried to find everything they had written about us, in case there was some evidence against me, but I found none.

On Herkulesgatan Nanna was huddled against the wall of the bank reading a book, her white hair like a curtain shielding her from the world. She had always looked at me as if she were seeking the good in me. No-one else did that, they were all trying to find the bad.

"Come on, love, let me warm you up," she said, stretching out her hand.

"You won't go, will you?" I said.

"Leave you? Never."

It was the last time I saw her.

For nine months I took almost nothing. I slept most of the time, lying under the window, half dreaming. Shane came and went and at night he lay behind my back with his hand on my stomach, as if sheltering the little creature inside from us. He kept falling asleep everywhere and was just getting thinner, even though we ate at McDonald's every day. It happened fast, he went away for a few hours and when he returned he was thinner still, as if something were consuming him from within. At night I dreamed about an animal that was eating him alive. It was huge and black and lay like a shadow behind him in the bed where I used to lie and hold him. He slept more and more and when his own clothes no longer fitted, he started wearing my jeans and jumpers.

Shane lay and listened to my stomach, a small, hard womb protruding like an egg from my soft belly. I thought about Valle all the time, that he would be reborn. The idea intensified the longer time went on, that he was the one growing inside me. Somehow he had turned up inside me again; I had been given a new chance and no-one knew. At the social services office I scarcely listened to what they were saying about him. They could say whatever they liked about the little community by Storsjön, about the people who had taken pity on him. Because only I knew that he was with me. I tried to tell Shane once, but it made him angry and he shook me by the shoulders. It hurt, not so much a physical pain, but that he didn't believe me. He had always believed me, he had always defended me and what I thought. So I was alone in my belief it was Valle. Perhaps I knew it wasn't true, but I entered that fantasy like walking into a room.

Later we were allowed to go to Jämtland to visit him. On the train I wasn't thinking about where we were going. Inside I was vacant. I had showered, made myself look nice, put on makeup, worn a coat with a fur collar. I couldn't fasten the coat over my stomach, but it was thick and looked good. I felt grown-up in it. The landscape was unreal; outside the city the sky was so wide, it was everywhere. It was a long time since I had seen a sky, for there were none in the city, you could catch an occasional glimpse of a pale blue square and then it was gone.

Now it stretched without end beyond the train window, as if we were riding through it. Maybe at that point I was happy, the baby's unhurried movements under my ribs were a world of its own, untouched by any danger.

Shane muttered to himself the whole time and walked back and forth down the train. As soon as he sat down he sprang up again, as if he had burned himself on the seat. I was calm, for me there was nothing at stake anymore, everything was inside me. The people were waiting at the station. They drove us into the country in an immaculate, newly washed car. They chatted to us, were unbearably gentle and kind, as if they were being paid. Well, they were. My fur coat looked a wreck on their pristine seat.

"How was the journey? It's a long way."

"How lovely to meet you."

"We've baked some buns."

"I think he might be a little bit shy at first."

"But we've plenty of time."

"Maybe you're hungry."

On the way I started to feel afraid; I couldn't cope with all the friendliness, I had no way of dealing with it, my entire repertoire was built on self-defence. We sat in the back of the car in silence. I was scared my voice would sound too loud and harsh if I said anything, like a chainsaw obliterating everything in its path. Shane answered their questions anyway, but his voice was thin and adrift and the words kept ebbing away before he could finish his sentence. They obviously knew we were expecting another child, but they didn't mention it. They must have thought we were idiots. If they did, I could only agree. We drove past something that looked like an ocean; they said it was Storsjön. They said Valle had been bathing in there all summer. It was as if they were talking about someone who had nothing to do with me. My Valle was floating in amniotic waters again.

We stepped out of the car at a yellow wooden house by the lake and a moment later I would come crashing out of my dream. We walked slowly through a garden and into the house. There were children's things in the garden, a little bicycle and a blue tent, and there was a small sandpit filled with buckets and spades. Valle was sitting on the floor playing when we entered and he didn't look up. An elderly woman was sitting at the kitchen table. He had grown taller, even though only a few months had passed, and he was wearing clothes I had never seen. Someone had cut his hair short and it was shining in the bright sunlight. I stood at the door and looked at him. Shane did too. The baby must have been woken by the sound of my heart and it made such an energetic movement, it had to have been visible through my jumper.

"See who's here, Valle."

Valle looked up. What was in his eyes? I don't know. The baby moved inside me and it was suddenly quite clear that it wasn't Valle who was hiding inside, waiting for us to become other people. He was sitting before us on the floor, utterly real, in jersey dungarees, in that yellow house where the light streamed into all the rooms like water.

After a while he walked up to us. A little while later he sat on my knee and ate some biscuits. It ought to have made me happy, but it only made me sad. His hair smelled so sweet, as it always did, like kitten's fur. I wept so much I made it wet. He patted me on the cheek and then he wanted us to walk around the house. Everything was perfect, like a doll's house. He had his own room with yellow walls and brightly coloured cushions on the bed. Later, when he wanted us to go outside, the sun was so strong I could hardly see. When we left he was sitting on his little bike, waving. Beside him stood his new parents, their big wings folded around him.

Autumn came and the one inside was growing and in time she started kicking Shane's hand with her tiny feet. Shane sang a little tune to her and I could feel her quietening down. One day without any forethought I said:

"When the baby's born we're going to take her to social services."

Shane's eyes glazed over.

"You're just frightened. We'll manage it this time. We're different people now."

"Aren't you frightened?"

Shane's hand cradled the baby in there more firmly.

"It's good to be scared. You said that yourself. That way you shape up."

"But we're not shaping up, are we? That's the thing with us – we don't shape up."

"Someone has given us another chance, I know it. Wait 'til you see her. It will all be different when she's here. She's going to bring *us* up."

It is a human weakness, overestimating your own capacity for change, it doesn't just apply to addicts.

Some distance away from Herkulesgatan the murderer was already setting the wheels in motion in his daydreams. Like a prisoner of himself he was driving back and forth along the roads looking for something, animal or human, girl, child or woman. He had no idea yet who I was, but he knew what he was looking for and I fitted the description. Someone going through life like the living dead, someone who no longer believed in salvation. A cold wave rose up in him at the thought, until finally it was all that was left in his soul. I imagine it is the same with the heroin that fills every artery and every nook inside you. Soon our paths would cross. It would be an accident, and yet not; it would be the last event in a long chain of chance events that are called a life. One night I would be standing in front of him on Herkulesgatan in my fox-fur boa.

I bought that boa after I had given birth to Solveig. And I finally acquired a short black skirt and a pair of high silver boots. Every time I caught a glimpse of my reflection in a shop window I wanted to laugh. But at last I knew who I was: I was just the picture of that figure in the reflection, the woman in the fox-fur boa. It was clean as a cut, and it was true.

The labour pains were much worse with Solveig. But I wanted to suffer the worst of all pains. I didn't want her to come out, so when it was time I refused to push. Shane had said he would only accompany me as far as the hospital doors and then he would go. Unless I changed my mind, as he put it. But he only said it to make it harder for me, it had been arranged long before. We had both already signed the documents and it couldn't be changed now, and besides, even if we kept her, in the end they would take her, in a year or two. This way she would be spared that. And so would we. So when it started – it was in the morning just after we had woken up – we took a taxi to the hospital. And it happened quickly this time, in half an hour I was on the floor groaning, blood running between my legs. In the taxi Shane held my hand tightly the whole time and every time I was gripped by a contraction he held on to me. He helped me out of the car, gave me my little case and my handbag and I walked towards the entrance on my own as the taxi door closed behind me. But I had only walked a few metres before I was seized by the brute force again and sank to the ground. Shane was back at my side, he picked me up, the only thing in that disgusting hospital environment that smelled good. He carried me up to the ward and I was hanging around his neck, and for a moment, between the pains, we laughed at ourselves in the stark, grainy light of the lift, at me the weight of a whale and him thinner than ever, and then, when I was lying in a bed in a hospital gown, he left. I would have left as well if I could, to escape the last bit. They might as well have put a little bowl under my fanny for Solveig to drop into and drown straight from the womb.

Deep down I had been hoping she would never come out, that time would be frozen and she would stay inside me forever. The only time I felt whole was when I had a child in my belly. That was why they had to use a ventouse to get her out. In the end a doctor stood between my legs, pulling on the traction chain until he was red in the face. The pains had long since subsided, it hardly hurt at all now, and I thought it was better for her to die in there, so that she could skip being born and I could be her grave. But in the end something deep inside came loose and burst out of me. Solveig's head had a scratch and a bump, but it was still small and round and beautiful. I breathed in the scent of newborn baby; I said her name was Solveig, they had told me I could decide; they stitched me up between my legs and left us on our own. Gradually the room around us filled with a cold, pale winter light that settled on her face. Soon the sound of footsteps and voices would be everywhere, but first it was just the two of us. The final moments are mine and Solveig's alone.

There are certain images you have to keep to yourself, or they will disappear; you have to keep them within, unalloyed, untouched. You have to try to ensure that the words don't destroy the pictures so the clarity and pain are lost. It doesn't matter that they hurt, as long as they are pure as glass.

"Doesn't she want to say goodbye?" I heard someone whisper in the delivery room. No, I didn't want to say goodbye to Solveig; no matter what I did, they would still have taken her from me. The only thing I had left to give her was to surrender her, instead of tearing her tiny pink body apart. As we had done to Valle. As we had done to one another. To God and the Devil and everyone else, I say: The one who loves a child most can also give it up. So I lay with my face to the wall and heard their whispering voices retreat down the corridor. And when they had taken the thing that until moments before had been as much a part of me as my gut, I picked up my belongings and walked out. The fur jacket, the bag, my book and my bicycle key. The milk seeping from my breasts was grey, grey as dishwater, as if my body knew no child would ever drink it. Soon I was sitting on a toilet floor in Central Station with a needle in my thigh. I never saw Solveig again.

It is the final days. We are still roaming around the city where the water lies dark and motionless between the islands: he, the man who is soon to strangle me, and I, the person I was when there still was a me, when I had a living body, when I still had time, when I still had children. I don't really believe I ever stopped bleeding until I died that summer. I still do have children, but they're not with me. They weren't with me at the end either, but I will always be Valle and Solveig's mother. Death can change much, but not the fact that Valle and Solveig came from my body. Maybe there are other people, like Ellen and Johan in Jönköping, upgrading them both to new and better versions now, but they originate from me.

We will meet soon. He has already seen me, but I haven't yet seen him. And now I watch myself walking along the streets that are shiny with spring rain, and I am searching for Shane, because he has disappeared again. We saw each other in April in Klara churchyard and he said it was a crime against nature to give Solveig away and then he never came back. I didn't know then it was the last time I would see him.

"I miss you," I said, but I didn't dare touch him as he sat leaning against a gravestone.

"Do you?"

He seemed surprised and kept looking around as if he was expecting someone.

"Are you waiting for someone, Shane?"

"I always am."

"I mean someone in particular?"

He shook his head but didn't answer. I was the only one speaking.

"Every time I wake up I think you're there and I reach out for you. Then I remember that you've gone."

"Where is she?"

"I don't know. Somewhere."

He fell silent and picked at the grass. I looked at his hands while I spoke. His wrists were so thin and pale. The tattoos had faded.

"But she's alright where she is. You and I can't have any children. I know that now."

Summer is almost here now and I still believe I am going to find him, even though I think he is wrong about us and Solveig. It is the only thing I have to hold on to, that the reason we didn't keep her was because we wanted her above all else. But Shane will never forgive me and actually it doesn't matter, he will never come back, because now time is up. As I walk along looking for him, I finally realise how awful it is to wander around asking for someone, when you should know where that person is. Shane told me so many times.

"Do you understand how humiliating it is when you have to ask around for your girlfriend?"

"Wife!"

"Yes, but what bloody difference does it make if we're married when I don't know where you are?"

"It matters to me. I know I'll always come back, even when I walk out on you."

"Oh, right, am I supposed to be happy about that?"

"I think so."

"The worst of it is that I am."

"What?"

"Happy when you come back."

And the person who is about to take me out of the world is going to and from work, where he has a lot to do, because he is at the age when you do have a lot to do, when you have a career, and for a while now he has been preoccupied with me. It makes him distracted and absent-minded, but also wide awake, and he moves through the days as lightly as air. For some time he hasn't known what to do with the energy that fills him. He already dreams about me at night, a recurring dream, of lifting my head off my neck, as easily as with a doll.

The first time he saw me must have been on Herkulesgatan when he drove past in his car. What is it about my appearance that makes him want to kill? That I am already dead, that I won't defend myself? In his imagination he marks out the lines on my body where he plans to make his cuts. The idea of my neck pleases him most, the mere thought of tightening his hands around my throat makes him gasp for breath. His fantasies about me guard him against the abyss, how he will let the light fill my eyes and the oxygen rush through my blood one last time, before he squeezes again. In this he is like the gods who play with us for a spell before they let us go. And the choking is nothing new. Practically every man nowadays wants to have his hands around your neck when he comes; I don't know where they got that horrendous image from. But it makes them come straightaway. And when they come they shout for God. Sometimes working the streets really is like being in a bloody church.

He watches me on Herkulesgatan from a distance. Perhaps he has been standing there looking at me many times already. I ought to drop this question and let it go, but it keeps coming back: Why did he choose me? I will never know. Does it matter? At any rate this is the first occasion we speak to one another, because suddenly he is standing beside me with his pale eyes and I think he is shorter than I am, but it might just be my high heels.

"Good evening," he says.

Summer fog used to be treacherous and we were driving into it now, fluffy and soft from a distance, as if it wanted to protect the world from something awful. As we drove into it the light disappeared and the air surrounding us became cold and raw and dark. The mist swallowed every sound, it sucked in the birds' cries and the hum of the overhead cables, and you were filled with a vast emptiness without knowing where it came from. We drove into the mist and there was no way back.

I looked at him sitting next to me, motionless as a sculpture in the last dim light. I knew I had reached the end, there was no point in running this time. Did we say anything, or did we sit in silence? Does it matter? We drove into the mist as if it were an alien world and a few hours later he would return alone.

"Are you really not scared?" he asked.

"No, I'm not scared."

"Not of anything?"

"Only people who hope for something are scared, and I don't."

He was quiet for a moment and then he said:

"You can tell a mile away that you're not afraid of anything. That you don't need anyone at all in this world."

"I did once. But that was a long time ago."

He gazed out of the window, his voice quite soft.

"The hardest part of killing someone is having to put out

the light in their eyes. But once you make your mind up, it's as easy as flicking a switch."

I said: "Throw my things into the river. I don't want there to be anything left of me in the world."

I went on: "And one more thing. Don't drag it out. Don't hurt me more than you must."

When he finally pulled up by the little slope leading down to the lake, it wasn't the car that stopped, but the world outside, for it seemed as though we continued our journey while the rest of the world stood still, waiting, holding its breath, like a tide that would suddenly turn. I fell backwards through time with him by my side, down to its very beginning. The church service was still coming out of the radio, but it was fainter now, I think they were playing Stabat Mater and the windscreen wipers swept slowly across the glass and it really did seem that we were falling together, downwards in time, and suddenly I was a mother again and I sat in the delivery room with Solveig in my arms. She still smelled of blood and vernix and then she was gone and a little boy who was Valle lay next to me in the narrow bed on Sockenplan, his hair soft and downy, sweaty with sleep and sun, and then I wasn't someone's mother anymore but I had found Shane, he was standing in front of me on Rådmansgatan and I stopped and threw a coin in his cap, and I was drawn to his world, like a magnet. But then he was gone too and I was a girl again in Alvik and I lay on a car bonnet beneath a slender silver moon with the sense that I bore the universe within me. And I carried on falling and there I was again, further back in time with Nanna and I had the first syringe in my hand, and quivering on its tip a crystalline droplet, translucent as a little mirror before it burst, and I can see now, as clearly as through a magnifying glass, that it never was a choice, it was something else, something inexplicable, a breeze or the breath of an unknown being passing through me, a moment of greater clarity than any other. And then I was back by the river under a yellow sky, kneeling in the cold water with Eskil in my arms, his little chest still, his eyes pale and motionless, and then, like a miracle in time's reversal, I was a big sister again and I lay in a large bed with my nose pressed to the milky fragrance of his soft neck while Raksha and Ivan bellowed at each other with the force of wild animals for whom love was forgotten. Then I see them again, Raksha and Ivan, and now just the two of them, as they looked when they met for the first time at a funfair in Ängelholm. She who would one day be my mother wears an A-line coat and Ivan has a beer glass in each hand and in the background a bluish landscape rolls out under the sky like a glittering map. Inside those two simmers something unknown, and it might be happiness or the first hint of sadness, but whatever it is, this is the way it feels when life eventually begins, and you have waited for it for so long, for something to happen to you, and I think Raksha has been waiting for something that will uproot her from her old world. And now it starts, with a kiss, in front of the giant yellow Ferris wheel that has been shunted around Sweden all that summer in the late '50s.

I will never know where she comes from, Raksha, what darkness she travelled through to reach us. All I know is that she moves in with Ivan after the first night, that the past is a firewall of black inside her. Beyond the wall lies all that was once burned away by a mighty conflagration.

This is my last picture of the world and it is of Raksha and Ivan, the world's starting point and its beginnings, and all the time he sits in the seat beside me, the hunter, and he watches me. And not only time stops in the end, but we stop too, and everything around us is still, a world of rain and dark water falling gently through the trees, and we have reached the place that is to be my grave.

His hands tightened around my neck like a rope, his face and hairless chest pressed against me. I couldn't breathe, my lungs gurgled as the air sacs burst, I tried to cough, I saw things. Maybe they were apparitions; I think it was the Virgin Mary again, when the angel visited her, and now I could see how frightened she was, how she imperceptibly backed away towards the wall, and I saw the angel rape her, saw it hold her hands to the ground and ejaculate into her, I sensed the smell of death on them, sweet and cold and stale. And now the seed plunged into her soul with its fearful tidings. She would bear a son and lose him. She would be given a child who would be killed before her eyes. For what? I will never believe that Mary understood. I will never believe she accepted her fate.

Then I saw myself, I saw the grey foam bubbling out of my mouth, a mixture of earth and blood and ragged mucous membranes. I saw myself lying on the black mud, naked, twisted into a strange position that made me look like a plucked chicken or a doll someone had thrown away at childhood's end. A streak of blood on my cheek, my eyes wide open but extinguished. I remember thinking I didn't want Raksha to see me like this, I didn't want anyone to see me, I never had.

But I can still see those children Eskil and I were, as we ran together beneath a pale sun, a piece of silver in the sky burning through the haze, a sun shining on two children who were all alone by the river under the great heavens, running. They are alone in the world, those two children, and when I watch them now the rest of the world has receded like a tide, waiting, quivering and quaking, in the grip of the moon before it starts to trickle back in microscopic rivulets that soon will fill the world. Such is grief, threatening at any moment to fill the entire world with its stinking black water. The children's bodies are white and naked against the inky silt on the shore and she, the girl who once was me, is always slightly in front, and the boy running after her is so very small in the wideness of the landscape. And if you zoom in on him you can see he has freckles, a shower of pale dots on his chest and arms. And he has little bags under his eyes, small folds that are always there because he struggles to sleep at night. If you zoom in even closer, you can see that his eyes are bright green, a special green colour that exists nowhere else in the world apart from in his eyes and in the Kattegat seen from heaven. I go there often to see that shade of green again.

"Is that you, Raksha? . . . Is there anybody there? . . . My head aches so much . . . I have so much pain all over . . . Where is my head? . . . Please help me get my head back . . . Was someone shouting for me? . . . Raksha, were you calling for us? . . . We're here! On the black shore under the heavens . . . Now the tide is coming in . . . It's washing over us . . . Raksha! . . . Mamma!"

"Don't shout," he whispers, and his face is closed like a marble statue's and there is nothing that scares me more than the stillness. It is the ones who are calm and never get angry who are dangerous, that I have learned on the street; they are the ones who do terrible things in private. I see the predator in him, the silhouette moving slowly like a shadow that I could reach out now and touch. And the words pour out of me and I can't stop myself.

"Please, please, please don't kill me. Don't hurt me."

This is the moment he has been waiting for, when I finally beg for my life. "Get onto your knees," he says. I kneel in the mire. He presses his thumbs on my throat and squeezes.

He let me return for a second before he gripped my throat with his hands for the last time and held on. The iridescent green light in the forest gloom came back once or twice, and the sound of the birds, before they disappeared forever.

SNOW

At my funeral it was snowing, the whole world was covered in a thin layer of snow, and when Ivan came walking up to Bromma church it looked as though it had been snowing inside him, for now he was quite silver-grey.

"Hello, Ivan," Raksha said, waiting on the church steps with a little bunch of flowers in her hand. When they walked together along the rows of pews, they could have been a young couple about to be wed, but they weren't. They were already married, and they had never been young. There were only the two of them there, apart from the priest and the organist and a sexton who stayed in the background. They sat right at the front and listened to the priest talk about the battle between light and darkness. From above Raksha and Ivan looked like two children in the large nave, sitting, their heads bowed. As soon as the music sounded, Raksha started to weep. She wept noisily, her mouth open like a child, runnels of snot and tears dripping onto her knees. Ivan took her hand and held it in his. Her legs shook and jerked like a panic-stricken deer.

When it was over they followed the gravedigger to the grave. A cold sun on the snow, the air clean and raw. A few snowflakes swirling around.

"Are you going home now?" she asked, while they waited.

"Yes, I'm going home now."

"It must be windy there by now."

"It's always windy there."

She wrung her cold hands.

"I was never very good with all that wind."

"Neither of us was particularly good at anything," he said, looking down into the hole that was to be my grave. That was the way it had been. They hadn't been particularly good at anything.

My body, or what was left of it, was lowered into the ground. Ivan thought Raksha would try to throw herself into the hole after me, so he kept his hand on her arm, but she stood perfectly still, staring ahead. The white coffin was lowered into the frozen ground and the grave was filled with earth. Outside the church they took each other's hand, and then they parted forever.

After all those years Raksha filed a petition for divorce. Ivan signed and returned it to the authorities. She was in the bath when she opened the letter declaring them to be divorced. She slid under the hot water and retreated into herself. Whatever it had been, it was over at last. She took her pills again and the old world opened up inside her, the world no-one else had access to, the one that was gentle and beautiful and light. Ivan sat on his balcony in the sun in his hat and gloves, waiting for spring. He sat so still the birds mistook him for a lifeless thing or a piece of furniture and would settle on him for a while. There he sat, waiting for the end to come.

There is still no stone on my grave. A simple wooden cross has been there all this time. Raksha has always intended to organise a stone, but it hasn't materialised. Every time she is there, she thinks she is going to arrange for a gravestone, but the years have passed and become decades. Before she leaves she usually kisses the grass growing on my grave. I have seen her kiss the snow. Sometimes she talks to me and occasionally might castigate me, but that is alright, I deserve it. Sometimes she sings a song in her rough, gravelly voice.

Little Raksha, an old lady now with silver hair, lying on her flower-patterned kitchen sofa all day long, deep in her half-dreams. She always has done this, I suppose. From death's perspective, life appears to be a strange dream without logic, so for me her daydreaming is starting to seem less peculiar. But the other day she suddenly rose from the sofa and took the turquoise telephone receiver down from the wall and ordered a gravestone, as if all she has ever done is order gravestones. She must have worked it all out long before, because in an instant she has the telephone number on a piece of paper in her hand. The statute of limitation has elapsed and they will never exhume my remains now. She said on the telephone that she hadn't decided yet what should be on the stone, but she knew it had to be rough-hewn and simple and that my name had to be in gold. And also, she added quickly when they had finished and were on the point of hanging up, and so quickly the man at the other end could hardly hear, it had to have this on it too:

HERE LIES THE DAUGHTER OF A HAIRDRESSER

Crazy little Raksha. She has never been a hairdresser, at least not a professional in a proper salon with a trolley full of expensive hairsprays. She cut my hair and Eskil's and Ivan's and did some of their friends and a few neighbours by the river and, later, on Svartviksvägen and she still cuts Sylvia's. Just imagine this is the epitaph she has been working on for the last twenty-five years. But perhaps she was only thinking that my profession wasn't appropriate for a gravestone, even if I had nothing against it myself. It is the truth, and it isn't any less true for being unseemly. Besides, you are allowed to lie on gravestones. People lie all the time, about everything, and especially on gravestones. *Greatly loved and sadly missed* it often says, although it isn't true. Sometimes it does become true after death, as it has for me and Raksha to a certain extent. After my death something between us eased and suddenly she could cope with me, maybe even love me. And I have always loved her, I still do, in the same way I did as a child, even though here those sorts of feelings fade over time. I still like seeing her small brown hands and the floral housecoats she lives in, the same ones she had when I was young. When she lies in her bath with a tiny angel on the rim and blows one smoke ring and then a second into the first, I think she is sending a little message to me and to us, those who were once her family.

Love is like snow coming to swathe the world in its light, and then it vanishes. I look for Nanna but she is hiding, as always. Until one day I see her on Herkulesgatan again. From above, her blonde hair gleams against the grey asphalt, the grey granite buildings. She is older and thinner, almost hollowed-out, but she moves as fast as she did before, as if the streets are hers and hers alone. She must have climbed out of a car because all of a sudden she is standing there next to a pillar, rummaging in a big bag. An old man glides up to her on a bicycle with a tape recorder on the pannier rack and together they walk down to Sergels Torg and on towards Klara churchyard.

Everyone on Herkulesgatan is always on the way to somewhere else, it is the only thing you talk about there, but no-one tends to get further than the morgue. I always thought Nanna would be the one to get away. Long ago she used to say she would take me with her to the great glacier at Kebnekaise, where there is no fear or dread, only light and sky and snow. We were going to take Valle with us and no-one would find us there. It didn't happen. I never saw her again after I had lost him, and the glacier is on its way out too, melting like the Russian tundra and Antarctica. Everything disappears, everything you love dies.

The day I came across Solveig alone by the dark stone in the churchyard was like dying again. Ghostly and thin in her coat, she looked so pale. She wasn't weeping, she was simply standing with her hand in front of her mouth, looking as though she was freezing on the warm summer evening. Clara stood a short distance away, leaning on a tree, smoking, looking at Solveig. After a while Clara walked up to Solveig and put her leather jacket around her shoulders. On the gravestone was his name: *Valentino*.

"Are we just going to leave him here among the dead?" Solveig's voice was small and hoarse.

"Yes."

"It doesn't feel right."

"It's what people do though, we just go."

You might be inclined to consider it a mistake, a temporary relapse, that he couldn't manage the same strength as before after being clean for so long, but I don't think it was. And a morphine death is gentle and kind, the sort everyone dreams of. I believe he had been alone for a long time and he didn't know what to do with all he was suddenly given, and maybe it was difficult for him to emerge into the light so abruptly, to find he had a sister like Solveig out of the blue. I know what hope can do to you.

*

Sometimes I think Ivan and Raksha were reckless people, careless about things that were important, lying for days by the water, drinking in the sun, forgetting all about us. But I believe it is just the same as Shane and me: you hope the children will save you, you forget they are so small, so helpless, so easy to harm when you call them forth from the shade of their unborn state with no comprehension of what you do.

Shane and I truly believed the children would save us, we told each other all the time: "When the baby's here, there'll be no more problems." How wrong we were. When the children arrive, the difficulties really start.

I returned to Herkulesgatan but everyone who had been there before had gone. Someone said Shane was in prison in Istanbul, someone else was convinced he was dead. No-one knew where Nanna had gone. It was as if there had been a nuclear war and only the nastiest people had survived. Many of them had been afflicted by that illness and it had all happened fast, they had instantly disappeared from the streets and been isolated in the major hospitals. That was where Shane was, though I didn't know it then, just a few thousand metres from Herkulesgatan where I was wandering around without him. He died only a few months after me, and just like me he ended up in a bag of sorts, a black plastic cocoon that they put straight into the ground.

I didn't attend any of the scheduled meetings with the authorities and I didn't write any threatening letters, I didn't complicate matters for any person on earth; the awareness that Solveig and Valle would be better off without us had finally sunk in, as a simple truth. And I didn't give it much thought, but I must have assumed it would be an overdose, that somehow it would happen naturally, in accordance with evolution, Darwin and all that. There is no gentler death.

I didn't deliberately run into his knife, I was running away from something else that scared me more than death, and he happened to be standing there with his blood-soaked dreams.

What was I running from? The short answer is that I was running from love. The long answer is far too long, and anyway there is no-one who bothers about long versions anymore. You are given only one chance, and you can never come back to this planet again. All that exists is the flickering little candle flame that is your breath. Look after that flame, Solveig.

When I looked in on you and Clara the other day I decided it would be the last time, from now on I am going to let you be. You are so beautiful and so grown-up, I am always slightly frightened when I see you. Next to you I feel like a child, for you are older now than I ever was. Possibly it makes me rather jealous. Not jealous as such, I would give you the stars if you asked me to, but when I see you I think I would have liked to be part of all that too. Love. Time passing without you thinking about it. The seasons. The weather. I would have liked to be grown-up, I would have liked to experience one more summer. I am sad that as soon as you found your brother, you lost him. But I believe you are strong, tough, like a tree. And the apple often falls far from the tree. Isn't that what they say, those in the know?

I am going to stop disturbing you now. Perhaps you didn't even hear me, but mistook me for a bird of the night or a grim story you once read in the newspaper. Don't believe everything you hear. And don't believe everything you think. Don't worry if people gossip about you and your origins. The brightest flame casts the darkest shadow. And you know, most of what I have gleaned about time and space and eternity is what I learnt listening to your lectures at the university. And it is fortunate I am dead, for how would I dare speak to you, standing there in the stream of light through the high windows with your suit and your Elvis hair, making everyone listen to you? Your explanations about the origin of the universe actually comfort me most, especially the story you tell the students about the birth of stars. About everything once upon a time being gathered into one small particle that exploded one day, about stars being formed from a vast exploding cloud of gas and then the stars themselves exploding and the heat producing carbon and oxygen and nitrogen and everything needed for you and Valle to come into being someday inside me. The same substances, as it happens, that are involved in the decomposition of a body and turn it into stardust. Accounts of how the universe continues to expand make it easier for me to let go, the thought that we are part of the same state of perpetual motion. I think, whatever happens to us, it has been only one second in eternity.

"So let us keep fast hold of hands, that when the birds begin, none of us be missing."　EMILY DICKINSON

A NOTE ABOUT THE AUTHOR

Sara Stridsberg is an internationally acclaimed writer and playwright whose work has been translated into more than twenty-five languages. A former member of the Swedish Academy, she is a leading feminist and artist in her native Sweden and around the world. Her novel *Valerie: or, The Faculty of Dreams* received the Nordic Council Literature Prize and was long-listed for the Man Booker International Prize.

A NOTE ABOUT THE TRANSLATOR

Deborah Bragan-Turner is a translator of Swedish literature and a former bookseller and academic librarian. She studied Scandinavian languages at University College London, and her translations include works by Per Olov Enquist and Anne Swärd.